D1629678

THE NEW FRONTIER

THE NEW FRONTIER

Reflections from the Irish Border

Edited by

James Conor Patterson

NEW ISLAND

THE NEW FRONTIER
First published in 2021 by
New Island Books
Glenshesk House
10 Richview Office Park
Clonskeagh
Dublin D14 V8C4
Republic of Ireland
www.newisland.ie

Compilation and Introduction © James Conor Patterson, 2021

Individual contributions © Respective authors, 2021

Print ISBN: 978-1-84840-816-6
eBook ISBN: 978-1-84840-817-3

'Helicopters', 'Don't Speak to The Brits, Just Pretend They Don't Exist', 'A Spider', 'North To The South', 'When I Land in Northern Ireland', 'Heritance', 'The Republicans' and 'The Family Reunion Show' are from *The Whole and Rain-Domed Universe* (2014) and *Self-Portrait in the Dark* (2008) by Colette Bryce, and are reprinted by permission of Picador. The quotation from *The Táin* in the epigraph to this book is from Ciaran Carson's translation of the poem, first published by Penguin, 2007. The Clare Dwyer Hogg poem 'Brexit: A Cry from the Irish Border' first appeared in the *Financial Times*, 2018.

Portions of this anthology, where indicated, are works of fiction. All incidents and dialogue, and all characters, with the exception of some historical and public figures, are products of the author's imagination and are not to be construed as real. Where real-life historical or public figures appear, the situations, incidents and dialogues concerning those persons are entirely fictional and are not intended to depict actual events or to change the entirely fictional nature of the work. In all other respects, any resemblance to actual persons, living or dead, is purely coincidental.

British Library Cataloguing in Publication Data. A CIP catalogue record for this book is available from the British Library.

Typeset by JVR Creative India
Proofread by Meg Walker, theperfectword.ie
Cover design by Niall McCormack, hitone.ie
Printed by Scandbook, scandbook.com

LOTTERY FUNDED

Gratefully supported by the Arts Council of Northern Ireland.

New Island Books is a member of Publishing Ireland.

10 9 8 7 6 5 4 3 2 1

MIX
Paper from
responsible sources
FSC® C021394

For my family

Is this how we should fight,
exchanging bitter words
like two groaning corpses?

– Cú Chulainn ('The Táin Bó Cúailnge'
translated by Ciaran Carson)

Contents

Editor's Introduction   1

1. Movement
Darran Anderson – 'Time Moves Both Ways'   6
Abby Oliveira – Two Poems   22
Peter Hollywood – 'The Cataracts Bus'   26
Nidhi Zak/Aria Eipe – 'On the Chances of Migrants
    Making it through Irish Port in a Truck'   36
Jill Crawford – 'What Crisp Water'   40
Lias Saoudi – 'The Mid-Ulster Male'   56

2. Language
Orla McAlinden – 'Anois Teacht an Earraigh'   70
Michelle Gallen – 'On the Wall'   86
Mícheál McCann – Three Poems   96
Luke Cassidy – 'A Good Turn'   104

3. Landscape
Maureen Boyle – Fragments and Poems   114
Garrett Carr – 'North South East West'   122
Dean Fee – 'Border Bars'   134
Jess McKinney – Six Poems   144
Marcel Krueger – 'A Topography of Wounds'   154
John Kelly – Three Poems   170

4. **Family**

Emily Cooper – 'Trees, Horses, and Dry
    Stone Walls!'   180
Kerri ní Dochartaigh – 'Faoi bhun Gloine/
    Beneath Glass'   196
Eoghan Walls – Six Poems   208
Maria McManus – 'The Silent Treatment'   216
Séamas O'Reilly – 'Sleepover'   234
Annemarie Ní Churreáin – 'Things I Know
    About My Father'   248

5. **The Old Ghosts**

Patrick McCabe – 'The Muffin Man'   262
Colette Bryce – Seven Poems   290
Conor O'Callaghan – 'The Duck'   300
Bronagh McAtasney – 'Chasing Boys
    through Woolies and Other War Stories'   316
Michael Hughes – 'Marcel Marceau'   326

INTRODUCTION

There's a saying in my part of the world that there's more than one way to skin a cat. That's *cat*, by the way, inflected with a *y* after the *c*, so that the cat you're likely to be skinning actually answers to *cyat*. The *y* in this case is illustrative of how even a common aphorism can move into the territory of a shibboleth. The north of Ireland is well known for such peculiarities, and once, they were even enough to have you shot.

By such minutiae [are] the infiltrators detected, Michael Donaghy reminds us. Borders need not be so complicated as those areas of transition where papers and passports are required. Borders are simply the dividing lines we create for ourselves, and can be as simple as an elongated vowel or as stark as a checkpoint with barbed wire and concrete bollards.

Indeed, just as there are many ways to skin a cat, so too are there many ways to cross a border. One example is how, after the Wall went up between East and West in 1960s Berlin, tunnels were dug. People have been known to risk getting shot or drowned on one of the many dangerous crossings from Mexico into the United States, and in the Mediterranean boats are capsized or blown out of the water.

Thankfully, this island's Border isn't nearly so precarious, though that hasn't always been the case. Up until 2003, entry into my *hometown* of Newry was conspicuously marked by a British Army watchtower on Cloughoge mountain. The nearby village of Bessbrook had the dubious distinction of hosting the busiest heliport in Western Europe, and in 1989 – the year my parents left for England – unemployment was similarly in poll position at 27.5%

For better or worse, I am a product of borders. Most of my family are from Newry, but circumstances were once so bad that my parents had to emigrate to Coventry where I was born. Not long after, we moved to Scotland, and in 1995 – a year after the first IRA ceasefire – we came home. My mother was interrogated for three hours by Special Branch when we arrived at port and there were occasions in the lead-up to our departure when my father discovered that his mail had been opened.

The contributors to this book are the products of borders as well. What form these dividing lines take depends on each person's circumstances, and their interpretations are many and various. For some, borders are personal; redolent of struggles with family or language, landscape or the body. For others, they represent much larger vistas, like history and war, poverty and race. For everyone, I think, borders signify boundaries to freedom, and it is only by challenging them through art that we can ascertain whether such boundaries are useful.

Personally speaking, the land Border in Ireland — enacted by Partition a century ago and wending its way unevenly between the pieces in this book — is emblematic of the sort of dividing line which has caused more harm than good. Other writers and editors might disagree, and that's OK, but it would be crass to feign neutrality on a subject which has shaped who we are, both as part of a collective, and as individuals.

The authors represented here are every bit as opinionated, and approach the concept of 'borders' with more fire, knowledge, compassion and variety than I could ever hope to muster in my own writing. And so I urge you: read them, enjoy them, learn from them. For theirs are the voices that school children in decades to come will refer back to for the impassioned, necessarily biased view of what Ireland was like at a crucial juncture in its history.

James Conor Patterson
Newry, May 2021

MOVEMENT

Darran Anderson grew up in Derry. He is the author of *Imaginary Cities* and *Inventory*. He lives in London.

TIME MOVES BOTH WAYS

They found gods everywhere, the first people to arrive here, after the ice had finally retreated. The world appeared new then, reborn. Each river had its own deity. Each mountain. Every natural feature. We would call them animists now, the people who named small gods. They invested every object with a living soul. My father, a hoarder, is the last of these pagan people. I am sifting through his possessions, mending broken items, sorting them into boxes while, several miles from here, he lies in intensive care. He has been at death's door for nine weeks now. Each object has its own god. The strange bed he is in. The phone through which we speak. The machine that breathes for him and keeps him from crossing over.

The window of my father's bedroom at home faces east. The river – where his mother and father both drowned – is visible as a silver sliver of light. This window is an object. It has a lifespan. It is not as old as the house. It was a replacement for one blown in by an errant IRA mortar. In another sense though, it is much older. It is made of sand. It was a beach once; every grain worn down by the sea, the wind, and the rain, across an unseen expanse of time. If, as the Celtic animists believed, every object has a soul or a little god, then windows do too. I think of them as cinema screens; possessing the memory of everything they have witnessed.

I rewind the footage. Most of it is uneventful. Cars going to and from the Border. People walking dogs. Once a year, a group of Orangemen march backwards along the Queen's Highway. The streetlights blink off and on. The constellations wheel, in a backspin, across the heavens. The sun rises in the west and sets in the east repeatedly. Seasons retreat. Winter follows spring.

The one constant in the footage is a vast oak tree to the left-hand side. As we reach back to the turn of the millennium, we slow the reversal. The scene begins to change. A checkpoint grows out of the ground; its broken pieces mended by the arc and contact of a wrecking ball. The tree is suddenly decorated with listening devices. A boy stands at the window staring out for the first time, towards the newly risen tower where a sniper – in turn – watches him.

Almost every day, we passed through that checkpoint. The local shop and pub lay on the other side. As did the 'Free State' and the promise of temporary escape from the Troubles in the wild sanctuary of Donegal. Almost every day, we passed through the zone, on foot or in the car, silent because of the unsubstantiated belief that they could hear everything you said. Slowing to a halt, my father was always addressed with the same patronising sneer, either with an English accent if a soldier or a rural Ulster Scots twang if an RUC officer.

'So where are we off to today, sir?'

'Home.'

'And where might that be then?'

Good question, and a wretched little seed to plant in someone's head.

I left home round about the time they were dismantling the checkpoint. We were glad to see it go, though glad is too positive a word. It was more like the feeling when a boot lifts from off your chest. The demolition was relatively painless. Further into town, the army base at Fort George took many years to clear. They had to decontaminate the land of heavy oils and arsenic, whatever the military were doing there. The next checkpoint over to ours, at Coshquin, had been dismantled in a much more kinetic fashion, when late one night the IRA forced a Catholic army base cook by the name of Patsy Gillespie to drive a van filled with explosives into it. They held his family hostage at gunpoint while others trailed him to make sure of their mission's success. The detonator was wired to the light that came on when he tried to open the door. Two other Border attacks were launched at the same time, with 'collaborators' of the security forces being used as human bombs. In South Armagh, a sentimental IRA member whispered to the victim not to open the van door but to climb out the window. To the dismay of their planners, these attacks failed to unite Ireland.

There was relief to see 'our' checkpoint vanish. The air felt lighter walking through the place where it once stood. For those of us with long enough memories, it still does. Yet we made a mistake in removing all trace of the checkpoint, understandable as that was. It is the classic paradoxical error of the iconoclast who topples the symbols of tyranny, only to erase evidence of them. Later, professional amnesiacs will come to say there never was tyranny, or resistance to it. And, sure enough, in the midst of Brexit brinkmanship, it was claimed there never had been a hard Border. What Border infrastructure was there, as Arlene Foster claimed, was merely for 'reasons of security and, even then, terrorists were able to come and go at their pleasure.'

'Well, who you gonna believe – me or your own eyes?' asked Chico Marx in *Duck Soup*. 'Well, who you gonna believe – me or your own memory?' asked the DUP. The amnesiacs succeed because although the past is objective, memory *is* subjective and therefore pliable. As Orwell put it, 'Who controls the past controls the future.' So just like that, in some colossal magic trick, a heavily militarised Border not only vanished but ceased to have ever existed to begin with. We should have left traces behind, rusting in the landscape. We should have argued in defence of ruins, but we were fools blinded by optimism.

Now that checkpoint exists in the memories of the shrinking generations who knew it. My young son will, with any luck, know little of that world of enmity and division. Yet you perform your own particular form of amnesia with your child, knowing that the soft world you are tempted to construct for them might rob them of the necessary armour needed to face the harshness of reality. How to equip them with decency but also resilience because you know all too well, and from within as without, that man is wolf to man.

There is so little left of the Border that journalists from elsewhere are reliant on road signs and different shades of tarmac for visual cues of where a kingdom ends, and a republic begins. Those of us who grew up on the Borderlands have our own signs, located throughout the landscape, yet even these are changing and prone to erasure. The concrete posts we wound our BMXs around are long gone, though the old crow roads they blocked are still there. The field where Amelia Earhart landed after a perilous solo flight across the Atlantic is the fourteenth hole of a rain-swept golf course. It is sobering to realise that so many years have passed that the little gatehouse where you had your first ecstatic kiss is now a ruin with the roof fallen in. Somehow hilarious too.

There is another place where our checkpoint still exists – the two-dimensional time travel of photography. Snapshots of my nearest, earliest architecture. The all-seeing watch-towers in Donovan Wylie's *Vision as Power*. Jonathan Olley's deeply embedded *Castles of Ulster*. The gloaming world of Willie Doherty's work, almost-secret places where fugitives slipped by and informers were taken for their last moments in this world. The old abnormals that were our normality, that were all we ever knew as kids, before we were turned out – prematurely aged it seems – into an unknowing world.

It doesn't matter how long you spend elsewhere. It doesn't matter that you've lived away for longer now than you lived there. It's still there; the tug of the feral. You feel it when the talk turns dark, and the drink turns bitter. You feel it passing through respectable cloistered worlds. You remember it the way bones remember fractures. I left home when *they* did, except neither of us really left.

All nations are fictions, but some are more believable than others. It is easy to believe in an island. It is just physically there, for one thing, and intact. To drive a schism through it takes work; physical work on the boundary but much deeper excavations too. There will always exist a yearning to be whole. How might one extract that from the desires and recollections of a population? One method is determinism. To convince people that it was always going to be that way, inescapable and irreversible. If successful, one might even persuade them that it *was* always that way. Structures help in this process. Institutions. It is a lot easier to believe in a border when it has all the vestiges of a state behind it – a civil service, a public broadcaster, security services. Coercion is always there, whether explicit or implied. It is amazing how easily consensus can come about when there is a gun barrel involved. Every display of military might is, however, also a statement of insecurity. So, appeals are made to higher powers. The divide must be recognised by other states; each engaged in their own border machinations. Every international acceptance makes the border less ephemeral. Yet the doubt remains, in rooms, in dreams. Are the unrecognised republics of Transnistria, Artsakh, Somaliland, Abkhazia, and South Ossetia any less real to their inhabitants?

The sky pays no notice to the Border. Birds pay no heed. Disbelief always threatens to break through, even in creatures as mighty and foolish as we are. Ideology is a useful ruse in making us believe in an invented border, but even true believers know that an *ism* cannot truly command the soul, short of breaking the mind or body of its possessor; and even then pockets of resistance will always exist, if only in the private decadence of thought. Identity is a much more compelling way to deliver it. Tie the Border to the way a person sees themselves and you will thread it intricately through how they see the entire world. Yet *who they are* is not enough. It must also be *who they are not*. Identity has to always be under threat for people to do terrible things to others and to themselves in the process.

Northern Ireland was an unwanted changeling. Even the father of Ulster Unionism, Edward Carson – a Dubliner fluent in Gaelic lest we forget – only begrudgingly accepted it as a last resort and not enough to accept the role of its first Prime Minister. Everyone had wanted a united Ireland, either an Irish republic or a British isle. The former had existed, as it happens, for a single day – 7 December 1922 – before Northern Ireland seceded by letter to the king.

Before Partition even took place, people were dying for this embryonic country. For one side, the forthcoming division was an affront, a wounding, and its agreement an act of treachery and abandonment that had already led to the slaughter of the Irish Civil War. On the other side, an ancestral last bastion perpetually under threat and men pledged their undying fealty to it. It did not matter that the pseudo-state was entirely invented. If anything, it fuelled this sense of fanatical loyalty, giving credence to the claim that fundamentalism so often has doubt as its malfunctioning engine. Both positions would exert a heavy death toll. I know of this violence – between the signing of the deal and the creation of the state – because my family were there. The stories were passed down. And with them came an object.

For a long time, I thought that the iron handcuffs had been dug up by my father; part of a whole host of items he had unearthed, from clay whiskey bottles to gas masks, working for the council. One day, waiting for a call from ICU about my dad, I sat inspecting them for markings, as a distraction, eventually narrowing them down online to one used by Victorian police.

'You know these handcuffs my da found?' It says here they were the type Houdini used in his escapes.'

'Those weren't your dad's.' My mum replied, 'Those were ours. We used to play with them as kids. Never found the key. They belonged to ... let's see ... he would have been your great great grandfather.'

Cornelius Doherty was his name. They called him Corny. I always thought my maternal grandmother's lineage was the one peaceful path in my family; the other branches of the family tree being full of British army veterans and war casualties, and members of the IRA who fought against the very battalions their fathers had served in. I thought this one line was peaceful because my grandmother had been a gentle lady, who died tragically young, but the truth seemed to be that no one back then had the luxury of not being involved in some way in one conflict or another. Corny was her grandfather. He was a well-known republican. When the Easter Rising was breaking out in Dublin, volunteers gathered, against orders, at his farm, next door to the now-vanished Watt's Distillery, intending to make their way south to fight in the revolution. The British authorities never forgot him.

There'd been trouble in Derry for years, but it exploded in 1920 with arson and pogroms, machine gun battles in the streets, snipers on monuments, accusations of government collusion and rumours of invasions of brigands from the hills. Catholics sailed across the river rather than risk the bridge, which had been seized by a unionist mob. As curfews and house raids were underway in the city, news arrived that Belfast too was burning. After two policemen were shot (Waters and Wiseman) in Derry near the quay, their colleagues in the Royal Irish Constabulary decided to take revenge on Catholic locals. Donning masks, ditching their uniforms but not their arms, they went on a spree of violence around the town. At times, it was indiscriminate, attacking whoever they met and at other times premeditated. They riddled Breslin's shop with bullets and tossed a grenade into the family home of a young rebel. They left a tobacconist and butcher's shop in ruins. My ancestor Cornelius was on their hit-list and finding he had vanished, they torched his farm, with the livestock trapped inside a barn. Those who heard the shrieking of the animals, as they burned in Corny Doherty's farm, remembered the sounds for the rest of their lives. I do not know if the act went avenged but I do know that shortly after, the rampaging extracurricular policemen, who'd been shooting at firemen, ran into a British Army patrol who mistook them for members of the IRA and shot three of them. The following year Northern Ireland was founded, a hundred years ago at the time of writing. The Royal Irish Constabulary became the Royal Ulster Constabulary.

Cornelius lived through that encounter to become an unwanting and unwanted citizen of the Northern State. A number of times, his survival, and thus the existence of his descendants – including myself – was a close-run thing. On one occasion, his home was raided. What transpired there is not clear, but he emerged with his life and a set of handcuffs that had been relieved from an RIC officer. The restraints were old even then. They were forged no later than 1870. I wondered what happened to the people that had once worn them and those who had used them, before the handcuffs had later changed into a kid's toy for nine Catholic children in a row.

If even an inanimate object is capable of transformation, it may be no surprise that a border could too. Yet it *is* surprising, given how much effort has been made – a century's worth – to convince us that the schism between North and South was, and remains, natural and inevitable. The truth is that the Border was created and contingent, and any number of alternatives were possible. Other possibilities *were* considered. It could have encompassed all of the traditional province of Ulster, swallowing Donegal, Cavan and Monaghan. It could have run along the Bann and thus saved the new state a lifetime of sectarian apart-hood and gerrymandering towards those west of that river. It could have left out Derry, parts of Tyrone, Fermanagh and Armagh, counting on pogroms to expel or corral Catholics in West Belfast. No border at all was a compelling possibility but one quickly discounted by anyone who knew the depths of man's oldest virtue and sin: pride.

Contingency gets wiped away. Everything in hindsight is made to bend to what came to pass, and other paths that were equally viable are ignored. History becomes an article of faith, predetermination. It happened thus so it was always going to happen that way; a view that runs entirely counter to the way we live our lives, with at least some semblance of free will.

Once the Border was made singular and laid down on the map, work got under way to make it appear real. Some efforts were inadvertent. Successive Irish governments ignored the warnings of W. B. Yeats that to make the state beholden to priests and bishops would drive a wedge in the country and they would never gain the North to which they still held claim. This reinforced the unionist fear of a papal island and fuelled an already burgeoning siege mentality. This, in turn, was costly for northern Catholics, given anything they obtained (the right to housing, the right to vote, the right not to be killed with impunity, etc.) would be seen as a zero-sum, fifth regiment threat to life and liberty in the last loyal bastion. Some efforts were more conspiratorial. It was not enough to have the North fear and hate the South. For the Border to truly exist, the South must reciprocate. So, it is alleged, MI5 colluded with loyalists on a series of devastating car bombs, killing thirty-four people, in Dublin and Monaghan. And sure enough, *nordies* travelling south of the Border soon found themselves receiving the 'cold hand' and hearing murmurings to keep their savagery 'up there'.

Truth is more slippery than facts suggest. It is not simply that this bordered land of ours could have been different. It *has* been different. Who remembers now that the North was once split into three at Lough Neagh between Oriel, Ulidia, and the Northern Uí Néill? Or that the sites of unionist heartlands were once within the kingdoms of Ulaid and Airgíalla? Who remembers the strange sea-straddling nation Dál Riata, which encompassed western parts of what is now Scotland and eastern parts of Ulster? Who remembers that time is fluid and that we are as much its creatures as we are of space?

Nations, like life, are always contingent. It could *yet* be different. Every insurgent knows that it is only treason if you fail. Republicans have known this since the French Revolution inspired their United Irishmen. The king-toppling revolutionaries of William of Orange knew it too. Legitimacy is retroactive.

After a quiet, distressing videocall with the hospital, I leave my mother to nap and wander along the Border, invisible as it is in the landscape. My father dwells now, clinging to existence, in another borderland, that needs no artifice or propaganda. The border between this world and the next. Or between this life and oblivion. I think of politics and maps, as a way of not thinking, as I walk across fields, through woods and along the lough shore. Perhaps we are condemned to be together on this island. Perhaps there is a kind of quantum theory of identity for those of us in the North, where we are both/and, and simultaneously neither. Perhaps there are checkpoints everywhere and the one we grew up next to was just the most overt manifestation.

I give in and let the wind and the landscape carry my thoughts away. They will be here aeons after we are gone, and the stories we have told ourselves and each other long forgotten. The heart-breaking fact of life – that nothing lasts forever – might also in different circumstances be a liberation. I reach a dry-stone wall separating the road from a field of crops. It has outlived the checkpoint it once passed through, and the visitors who guarded it. As have we. I remember walking along its ledge as a boy, lost in thought. I'm still there.

Abby Oliveira is a writer, performer, lyricist and theatre maker based in Derry. She performs regularly at events and festivals throughout the UK and Ireland, and has toured work internationally in Australia and Singapore. She has had work commissioned by BBC Radio 4, BBC Radio Foyle, RTÉ Radio, and more.

A MAP OF THE WORLD IN PRIMARY COLOURS

Our teacher unravelled the world one day,
stuck a thumbtack in Scotland's thick ear

declared us a pinprick on a pinprick
whizzing through space.

She showed us the nose of the Hebrides,
a chin in Kintyre, Arran, Islay,
the UK: cross-armed, hunchbacked,
a Victorian judge.

Iceland, an unshorn ram.
Italy, a couture boot.
Mexico, a witch's locked jaw.
South America, panther's tooth.
Greenland, the skull of an ancient seahorse,
The USA in its belly. Heart chambers,
the beat-up waves of Hudson Bay, Foxe Basin.
Mother Africa's afro, wrapped
from South Sudan
to the Atlas Mountains.

I can still see the koala bear in Ireland.
These days her necklace is a throat
slit by a dirty, blunt blade.

WHOLE

I thought I'd have to saw myself in half
to stand in two countries at once, says the wean,

jumping state
ropes on
the Border back-
road.

But I'm still whole.

Arms outstretched as if tied to a rack, she says
We're holding hands. Me, Donegal and Derry.

There's no here or there for her
yet.

No euro, sterling,
foreigner, citizen,
trouble, peace,
president, queen,
ally, enemy.

She is the flock of Brent Geese
breaking for Inch.

Should I have pointed out the invisible line? Told her
              to imagine a fat, sleeping snake
         only old people can see,
              three-hundred-and-ten miles from forked tongue
to rattling tail,
belly harrowing
                   through water, concrete,
         grass, stone,
                        hearts, brains,
         danger-houses,
                   homes?
Should I pretend this snake no longer bites?

All borders draw blood.
The pen   is
the master
of   the sword.

One too-young day
she will be old
enough to see

that walls are only necessary
until imaginations harden.

By then,
she'll have sawn herself
in halves, quarters, acres —
a thousand times over, yet
she will still be whole.

Peter Hollywood is the author of *Jane Alley*, Pretani Press (1987); *Lead City and Other Stories* (2002) and *Luggage* (2008), both Lagan Press; *Hawks and Other Short Stories* (2013) and *Drowning the Gowns* (2016), both New Island Books. He appears in three anthologies: *State of the Art: Short Stories by New Irish Writers*, Hodder and Stoughton (1992), *Krino, 1986-1996: An Anthology of Modern Irish Writing*, Gill & MacMillan (1996) and *Belfast Stories*, Doire Press (2019). Peter is currently Royal Literary Fund Writing Fellow at the Seamus Heaney Centre, Queen's University Belfast.

THE CATARACTS BUS

The Cataracts Bus from Cork City crossed into the North just as the sun was coming up over the Cooley Mountains. The elderly passengers on board were asleep and did not notice. Cassady was at the wheel.

At the motion of Cassady's head, Shane reached forward and adjusted the roller-blind to keep the sun out of the driver's eyes. Then he sat back, awake, alert, looking all round him. Shane had agreed the previous week to – as Cassady put it – 'ride shotgun' for him.

'So where's it at then?' Shane asked.

Cassady sighed. The questions had started as soon as the bus drove over the Mary McAleese Bridge which spanned the River Boyne. A few weeks off twenty, Shane had never been this far north before.

'You can't see it. It's not something you can fucken photograph.'

Shane had been sitting with his iPhone ready.

'But sure, then, how do you know?'

'How do you know what?' Cassady looked round at him.

'How do you know when you're fucken across?' Shane cursed in a stage whisper, on account of the old people within earshot, some of whom were beginning to stir.

It would have been easier back in the day, Cassady mulled. Back then there were police checkpoints, army-posts, observation towers and barriers of great blocks of concrete signifying the divide. He didn't bother saying any of this to Shane though. Instead he said:

'Sure haven't the people horns on their heads. And don't they eat their young?'

'Seriously,' Shane bridled.

'Different speed limits,' Cassady said, softening. Then, a little further along, 'Look.'

A large signpost was fast approaching on the verge up ahead. *Welcome to Northern Ireland*, drivers were informed. *Speed limits in miles per hour*. The signage was scarred, pierced, punctured.

'You're not going to tell me those were bullet holes,' Shane said, snapping the sign as they whizzed past. He'd promised Dervla he'd send photos.

'This here is South Armagh we're driving through,' Cassady said, '*Bandido Country*.' Shane used the words to caption the photo he pinged off.

'Welcome to Dodge,' Cassady drawled. As the bus continued on, its sensor became confused before the computer managed to work out the speed conversion and a noise started to scream at Cassady from the dashboard. They weren't long over the dividing line into Northern Ireland before they were met by roadworks. *Adverse Camber Slow*, a sign read.

As the bus's occupants waited for the Go signal, they could see the green onion cupola of Cloghogue Chapel in the distance to the right.

Shane started up again. 'Reckon there'll be a poll? A vote? About doing away with the whole fucken thing?'

'God,' groaned Cassady, jerking his thumb backwards toward the passengers. '*They'll* not fucken thank ye for one. Least not 'til they get their eyes done.'

Shane looked behind him. The passengers might as well have been pilgrims going to Knock or Lough Derg; to the airport, off to Lourdes or Fatima or Medjugorje. Instead, they were all taking advantage of the Cross-Border Healthcare Directive, a piece of EU legislation allowing them to avail of faster and cheaper cataract surgery in a private clinic in Belfast.

After moving through the traffic, the bus stopped briefly for a comfort break on the outskirts of Newry. Then further on, outside Hillsborough, Shane snapped his first flag; a Union Jack rippling in a stiff breeze.

*

The eye clinic was located on a commercial thoroughfare in south Belfast. With his hazard lights on, Cassady pulled up outside and told Shane it was time to earn his keep. Accordingly, Shane sprang into action, joking and cajoling and escorting the older passengers off the bus, offering this one a hand, lending that one an arm and guiding them all up the pathway and in through the polished, automatic doors. Cassady had a favourite parking spot in a nearby industrial estate. It was here he would relax and read the paper while his passengers all had their eyes seen to. There was a hauliers' caff to have his lunch in, then he'd nap until it was time to pick up his busload in the afternoon.

Shane, on the other hand, was here to widen his horizons. Handing him a twenty sterling note, Cassady urged caution on the lad.

'I don't want Meábh on my fucken back if something happens you.'

Meábh was Shane's mum, and he didn't care for the familiarity with which Cassady bandied about her name.

'I'm a big boy,' Shane told him.

'Well, even so. Keep your phone on,' Cassady said.

It was a busy road – an arterial route which fed into the City Centre – and Shane watched as Cassady merged the bus into the heavy traffic, a blaze of yellow registration plates, nudging in that direction.

Not expecting a war zone exactly, nor the Aurora Borealis, neither was Shane expecting a Bang & Olufsen showroom located opposite a Starbucks, or a laser-eye surgery beside Orchid Lingerie, outside of which he didn't tarry overlong. There were fine art and antiques shops and galleries. Health food stores and delicatessens. There were women in scarlet coats and pastel colours with blonde, blonde hair, laying down expensive contrails of perfume. They walked small dogs on retractable leads, and had poo-bags dangling from manicured fingers.

The road, Shane realised, was a wide and bustling divide. He saw how there were narrow, residential side streets on one side and wider, tree-lined avenues on the other. He turned down one of the side streets, and found himself in a grid of well-presented two-up-two-down terraced houses. Many had flags furled from their fronts. Coloured incisors of bunting were strung about the lampposts. On one gable end, his eyes lit up at the mural of a masked gunman. This he snapped and WhatsApped in one flowing motion before the twitch of a curtain in an upstairs window encouraged him to move along.

The door into the nearby Maude's café didn't close properly. A cardboard sign said *Shut Happens*.

A sprawling, gangly youth just inside the door looked at him and said, 'How you gettin' on, big lad?'

Shane heard his own, somehow disembodied West Cork accent answer, 'Grand. Just grand.'

An awkward silence seemed to ensue and Shane hastened to the counter where Maude was waiting. He knew it was Maude from the large, framed photograph on the wall behind her. In it, she had the sort of flag Shane associated with English soccer fans draped around her shoulders, and the caption below read: *For Maude and Ulster*.

Shane mumbled something about ordering a cup of tea, then produced the note which Cassady had given him.

Maude looked at it and said, 'Nothin' smaller, luv?'

'What?' Shane leaned forward a little.

'Have you not got nothin' smaller?'

'Oh. Right. Yeah.'

What loose change he had was in the palm of his hand before he could think, and gazing on the coins Maude enquired, 'You been abroad, love? Your holidays?'

Dumbstruck, Shane could only offer the note again.

'Y'awright there Maude?' The youth checked in, aware there was some sort of exchange occurring at the counter.

'Nothin' for you to bother yourself about, Dale,' Maude replied, all the time keeping her eyes on Shane.

'That'll be to go,' she declared before turning to get the tea.

Shane stood with the banknote limp in his hand.

'On the house,' she informed him. 'Lids are over there.'

Shane had difficulty finding a lid to fit his disposable cup. He didn't bother asking if there was any milk. Then, struggling to get the door open again, some of the tea sloshed over his hand.

'Keep her lit,' the youth called after him.

'Thanks, I will,' Shane assured him.

Back on the main thoroughfare, Shane caught something in the corner of his eye – a sight so familiar as to go unremarked elsewhere but causing him here to check himself and look again. A group of girls, jostling and joshing on the other side of the road in Gaelic tops. Meábh had forbidden him from wearing his club tracksuit. Not *up there* as she'd put it.

It took him a while to negotiate getting across the busy road, and by the time he had done so, the girls had turned down one of the avenues. Nevertheless, he managed to locate which one and duly followed them, only to find himself in the University area of the city. One girl wore a hoody with *Queens Gaelic Club* on its back. Not an apostrophe in sight.

Later that afternoon, Cassady beckoned him by text. 'Time to rock 'n roll,' he said.

'Still in one piece,' Cassady observed, when Shane arrived back on the bus.

'No sweat,' Shane answered. 'What was all the worry about?' He made no mention of Maude.

'Well,' said Cassady nodding in the direction of the clinic's foyer. 'There they are. Eleven Long John fucken Silvers. Go get 'em, Jim Hawkins.'

Accordingly, Shane went forward to lend a helping hand, and one by one, the one-eyed passengers got back onboard the bus. Those with patches on the right eye sat on the seats to the left and those with patched left eyes placed themselves on the right. Once they were on the road again, he texted Dervla.

No night guards, he said.

No wall?

There's really nothing at all.

'Is that your girl?' Cassady asked.

'What?'

'Your cushla. That who you're texting?'

'She's not my girl,' retorted Shane.

He was thinking about the Gaelic girls that afternoon and how, in the Students' Union café, he'd succeeded in making eye-contact and ended up joining them and having the craic. They wanted to know all about the County Cork. The two girls from Tyrone and one from Armagh and the pretty one from Newry.

Outside Banbridge, his eyes began to close, and by the time the bus had reached the signposts Shane had earlier photographed, he was asleep. Cassady looked around, alerted by the soft snore and the lack of questions.

The Cooley Mountains were barely discernible now in the dusk as the Cataracts Bus rattled south again. For it was out there all right, make no mistake: a line on the map/a line in the sand; a tightrope/a tight hold; a frontier/an affront; a part of a union/a partitioning; a centenarian/a centurion; metric for one side/imperial the other. It was enduring for some and unendurable for many; a thing almost innominate; and it was out there all the time, heedless and unseen, possessing as it does the invisibility of a virus.

Nidhi Zak/Aria Eipe is a poet, pacifist and fabulist. Founder of the Play It Forward Fellowships, she serves as poetry editor at Skein Press and *Fallow Media*, and contributing editor with *The Stinging Fly*. Her debut poetry collection, *Auguries of a Minor God*, is published with Faber & Faber (2021).

ON THE CHANCES OF MIGRANTS MAKING IT THROUGH IRISH PORT IN A TRUCK

That European birds migrate across the seas or to Asia was understood in the Middle Ages, but subsequently forgotten.[1]

With 1.3 million freight vehicles and trailers passing through the three main Irish ports annually, the Garda and the Revenue's Custom service face a mammoth task in detecting migrants or contraband, such as drugs and counterfeit cigarettes, being smuggled into the Republic.

Senior Garda officers in particular are very concerned that cases like the discovery of sixteen Middle Eastern migrants – all male and two of them juveniles – are about to become more frequent when Britain becomes harder to enter.

These birds go in large flocks, frequently of several hundreds, and commonly in parties of not less than thirty or forty together ... They are scarcely so suspicious as on the ground, where you can hardly approach them within a few hundred yards, and if the majority fly off first, a few generally 'wait a little longer'.

The Rev. Gilbert White, in his 'Natural History of Selborne', Hampshire, remarked [of] the large flocks to be met with in hard weather being almost exclusively composed of females. Linnaeus, in his 'Fauna of Sweden,' records his observation of the like circumstance there, and says that the females migrate from that country in the winter, but that the males do not.

The concern is that some will come here and apply for international protection with the ultimate aim of catching a ferry to Britain and disappearing there unnoticed and undocumented.

Gardaí believe Britain is a much more popular destination for illegal migrants and the numbers entering Ireland in containers are relatively small, though they have no way to be sure.

While trucks carrying freight are sealed when the containers are loaded, this has not stopped migrants, or the gangs that smuggle and traffic them, bypassing the seals, which snap if the truck's doors are opened.

In some cases, holes are cut in the roofs of refrigerated containers, or curtain-sided trailers are slashed with knives, allowing people to climb in.

Occasionally, however, two or three seem to withdraw from the main body ... Their thought may be to remain to breed, but for the most part, from some cause or other, it is doomed to be an abortive one.

In Ireland [the] occasional visitor has been noticed near Belfast, Ballymena, Lough Mask, Armagh, Rockland, Mertoun, Cork, Tanderagee, Antrim, Ranelagh, and Dublin, and in the counties of Wicklow, Cavan, Wexford and Londonderry.

These birds, as mentioned above, would seem to migrate in a north-easterly direction, and accordingly leave Ireland sooner than Scotland on their return to their native lands, and appear to choose moonlit nights for their flight.

They are said to be not at all shy in their native countries, but in fact all birds' natures are then temporarily altered more or less in this respect. They are capable of being kept in confinement.

In the case of the 16 males detected in a truck's trailer on the Stena sailing from Cherbourg to Rosslare on Thursday morning; one of the ferry company's employees heard the men inside the container and raised the alarm.

[These birds] are very vociferous, even in the depth of winter, so that the dejected face of nature is enlivened by their ceaseless notes, and likewise during their migrations a constant strain of conversation is kept up, which, as harbinging the return of spring, is a welcome sound even to those who are doomed to suffer from their ravages.

But what would have happened had the men gone undetected on board and still been in the container as it was driven off the ferry?[ii]

At this stage of the narrative ... I have arrived at that portion of my, alas! too brief, allotted space which is assigned to the subject of migration.[iii]

---

[i] Epigraph drawn from the entry for *migration (n.)* in the *Online Etymology Dictionary*.
[ii] 'What are the chances of migrants making it through Irish port in a truck?' *The Irish Times*, 23 November, 2019.
[iii] Morris, Rev. F. O. *A History of British Birds*. Volume III. London, Groombridge and Sons, 1870.

Jill Crawford grew up in County Derry, Northern Ireland. Her writing has appeared in *The Stinging Fly*, *n+1*, *Winter Papers*, and elsewhere. Her story 'Lambeth' was included in *Being Various: New Irish Short Stories* (Faber & Faber, 2019), edited by Lucy Caldwell. A novel is in progress.

WHAT CRISP WATER

In the 1990s, my dad travelled often through Ireland for his work in the quarries. If the Gardaí, from another piece of the island, ever caught him slightly erring in his driving, he might've looked all innocent and feigned ignorance in his most rural Northerly voice. 'Oh I'm sorry. I'm not from here and don't know the ways.'

During long summers, we'd gallivant by car over a border, across water: at least once with Antrim cousins to Bantry Bay, where in a borrowed wetsuit I learnt to sail those flimsy boats which require you, while changing direction, to duck under a sweeping boom and plant your weight on the other side to create a balance against the wind; on a different occasion, in caravans accompanied by a Ballyronan family along the west coast of Ireland on what we called the 'route de Dingle'; by a ferry from Belfast to Birkenhead on the 'mainland', then a good drive north for a tour of the Lake District; or by boat from Dublin to Cherbourg and descending to a Eurocamp site near Bordeaux, where we bumped into a Tyrone cousin in the showers.

My first solitary voyage was at about twelve when I flew on an exchange to Madrid. With me, I carried a hardback omnibus volume of *All Creatures Great and Small* by James Herriot. I stayed in the home of a Spanish girl, Mandy. At the supermarket, I discovered a brain, bright on a Styrofoam tray under cling film. They dined at 10 p.m.

My second journey alone was as part of the Ocean Youth Club, now Ocean Youth Trust, a charitable organisation which immersed young ones from 'all walks' in communal living and collaborative sail training. Alongside a skeleton crew and a group of teens I didn't know, from north and south, I sailed away for a week from Carrickfergus through light and mist to wherever our yacht was blown, in this case up the North Channel through the Hebrides and east along the Sound of Mull as far as Oban in the West Highlands.

It's true that I haven't flowed much to the west of where I was reared, and I barely know Derry City. My partner comes from there, over the Glenshane Pass; in future we may be intricately acquainted. According to an inquisitive aunt, the family of a great-granny-on-my-mother's-side hailed from Horn Head, a peninsula next to Dunfanaghy, a fishing port on the north-western coast of the island. I've never been to Horn Head. My partner tells me those cliffs are magnificent, harrowing. The plunge from road to water so appalled his mother that she leapt from the car and walked, only trusting her feet. Though north even of where I lived in the North, Horn Head belongs to the South, the Republic. This makes no sense and has its own logic. My great-granny would've been born there prior to the births of Northern Ireland and the Republic of Ireland, before separation.

All this is to say that while wading and bobbing through early life, perhaps because I lived a mere half-hour from the rim of the ocean on a brief island enclosed in a rolling, shining, opaque expanse of brave indefatigable salt water, I had a tingling awareness of being surrounded by numerous energies, many angles I might explore, real immaculate offerings. I could glide east to Belfast, England, Denmark, Lithuania, and all that Russia is; spill down through the Republic to Spain and Africa, where I'd already spent a while; turn west to Doire or Donegal, through which my family had passed, as far as America and Canada, where currents of this blood have reached, evaporated; drift north to the Hebrides, Faroe Islands, Iceland, Greenland, Svalbard, the withering Arctic where I'd never survive; pitch off an end of land into edgeless sea; rise through ether to outer space.

*

From primary age, I attended a swimming club in Magherafelt where I went to school and where my grandparents-on-my-mother's-side lived. We trained on Tuesday in the early morning and on Thursday evening.

After school on Thursdays, between hockey and swimming, my sister and I would go to the home of family friends. They lived on an old farm on the outskirts of town, opposite a field of horses, and were the only Protestant nationalist family of which I was aware (you don't always know). The children were fun, sporty, widely-travelled, well-educated, lovely, devout. For them, it wasn't even okay to say 'sugar!' instead of 'shit!' or 'Christ!', though they didn't insist I'd be damned for not believing as they did. We devoured heaps of toast with Panda Two Tone chocolate spread. We devoured warm potato bread with corned beef and cheddar cheese, melted in the microwave. We played Super Mario on the Nintendo. We played football on the crop of green in front of the ha-ha, which invisibly divided the lawn from the meadow, where they cut hay and grazed animals. We watched WWF matches on TV. The middle son, my age, had a pet snake. In their cabinet freezer, they stored frozen mice to feed it.

Their parents scarcely seemed to be there, always at work in the hospital that long ago served as the workhouse, where someone in my family had once lived and dissolved too young. There's a story here. We only know pieces. My inquisitive aunt wonders if this someone might've been a Catholic. In that place for the desperate and ashamed, dear ruined mother of the mother of my mother was submerged alone forever. That knowledge scalds my heart with a certain coldness. It popples through my stomach, lingers in the inability to trust utterly, in my refusal to allow bleak things to stifle the pleasure and freshness of being alive.

Why, yet, this love or pain on her behalf? It's imposs-
ible and real. Pieces of her life are tragic, revolting. I'm
not ashamed but indebted, indignant. My comrade! I'd
butterfly back against the tide of time to rescue her if I
could, but she crossed the brink and there is no returning.

On Saturdays, our swimming club participated in galas.
Another club would travel to us at the Greenvale Leisure
Centre, or we'd coach to them to compete in races, individ-
ual and relay. Sometimes we descended as far as Monaghan,
over the Border. No big deal. At the time I'd have called it
'down south'; it's part of Ulster but not part of Northern
Ireland. I wouldn't have said simply 'Ireland'. We were
Ireland, too. I was as Irish as anybody while also Northern
Irish, of the UK, and to be precise a country and Border-
county girl. This is intimate, particular. To each their own.

My granny-on-my-mother's-side called the South of
Ireland 'the Free State', a surprise to me since we were of
the sect that reflexively favoured Great Britain and feared
being sundered, so I couldn't imagine why she used that
glamorous name for the land over the crooked split, where
life was supposed to be different. Sure, these distinctions
weren't much more pronounced than those between vil-
lage and village, five minutes apart, where accent and
rituals might contrast. As a youngster, I didn't realise that
once upon a time there was no crooked split. It was nearly
as young as my granny.

In memories, I can't picture the Army at the Border
between North and South. I see armed checkpoints *within*

the North. Up our road toward the Glenshane Pass – an escape route in my imagination. At another edge of my hometown of Maghera. On the pinnacle of the mountain pass near The Ponderosa bar and restaurant. Was it? Into Tobermore, a Protestant village from which a portion of my family came. In the middle of Cookstown, where cousins lived. On the rural approach to Aldergrove Airport, now Belfast International. And elsewhere. Oh yes, in Toome, Coleraine, Randalstown, Kilrea, Holywood, Limavady ...

I recall men with machine guns outside school and up Queen Street in front of Mary's Bar, at the Diamond where the weekly market was. I feel cryptic and sinister bodies streaming through private gardens in darkness. 'Close them blinds or extinguish the light if you're at the loo in case the soldiers might be fit to gawk. Use a nice smelly candle if you're having a soak.' That was usual and has been recounted by those who were more exposed and who pre-date me.

Why then can I no longer see the Border checkpoints from North to South? They were very much there. They've dispersed. Accidentally and intentionally, for good and ill, I've tended not to dwell on minutiae of present or past. In that way, I am freer. There's been enough dwelling, I've often thought. Other times, I reckon we could do with listening and absorbing every detail, together paying attention once and for all in an attempt to let it pour out, perform a cleansing. It won't happen, not in my life. The freeze is overwhelming.

There's deep peril in releasing such splashy evils. You could be towed under. People do, see, hear and believe what they need. That's the height of it.

One border control that resides clearly in me was from 1996, my third trip without my parents. It was not within the island of Ireland. In my memory, we are in Strasbourg Airport. We've travelled here as a class with several teachers to visit institutions, such as the European Court of Human Rights. We are in Lower Sixth at a rare mixed-denomination school in the North, a Grammar, and we're undertaking European Studies. So far, we've learned about the foundation of the EU and EU citizenship, about the pioneers who inspired the EU project, and about its predecessors the ECSC, and the EEC. Though we're young Europeans, the border police won't let us through to start our adventure, our research.

We sprawl on the floor or wobble on luggage in an unsoft customs hall for what seems hours while armed Frenchmen grope through the contents of every bag. This is because we're from Northern Ireland. We, a muddled bunch of impatient rural schoolchildren, are a menace. It's silly and annoying. We get it.

I'm hosted by Nadège, a teenager from Strasbourg who lives with her mother and siblings in a flat within a large block. I've never been in a flat. We eat Ivorian food for supper, and they laugh when I make the typical error of refusing another helping by saying I'm *pleine*, pregnant.

While in Strasbourg, my slightly-magical French teacher, a Southerner, suggests I consider applying to a famous English university. A poet, whose brother lives on our road and who comes from a village ten minutes away, has recently occupied the role of Professor of Poetry there. I'm no genius, not even best in the year, but with him in mind I decide it mightn't be impossible, if I toil and am lucky. I don't expect it to be a simple endeavour. I've read *Jude the Obscure*.

For the duration of our visit, Nadège lends me her bed and sleeps. I look out a small high window at a rain-lashed city that's shifted nationality so many times and think how refreshing this France and these French are. Kids smoke in school. They don't wear a uniform. You call someone *spécial* to convey that they're weird. I wish everyone in the North and South could have this chance to come away from home, to another place, and begin to know it. Soon they'd realise how alike we are, who live on this island, despite our tiny variations. That's detritus and ephemera, unworthy of apocalypses.

In the last few years of being home, I studied three languages and forms of literature: English, French and Spanish. I was fascinated by language, how it reflected and pinned us while continuing to metamorphose, piece by piece.

At school, we were taught Castilian Spanish. I didn't yet know the myriad versions of Spanish spoken in Spain and across the planet, but I knew that in the

Basque country they spoke the Basque language and that in an eastern bit of Spain, containing Barcelona, they spoke Catalan.

We analysed a play by Federico del Sagrado Corazón de Jesús García Lorca. That name was gorgeous, pious, sensual, excessive. I perceived in it the idealistic yearning of adoring, fresh parents; later I found gullible devotion to an unnerved ideology that would find abomination in their son's manner of desiring, his reach for freedom and abundance.

In our small Spanish class, I sat beside a friend from my town, the only other girl. We attended the same church. I was more relaxed and unreliable about church-going. My parents gave me a choice, and nobody had offered good answers to questions that arose when I, a why child, had asked. Why are the elders only boys while wives just get to bake and decorate the church? How's it fair for somebody to go to hell if they've never had a chance to even hear of God and Jesus, never mind choose Christianity and be born again? Why can't others go to paradise if they're excellent: Mother Theresa, Freddie Mercury, the Japanese or the Māori who might worship alternate notions of the sacred? Isn't it vain to insist on being worshipped?

By the time I came to Lorca, my quandary had already been resolved when the Reverend said in Sunday School that it was sinful to go to Nero's Disco in Portstewart during the summer. Was it the alcohol, kissing, commingling of all sorts, dancing to alive, rude music when 'Born Slippy' and 'Rearviewmirror' were the thing? I couldn't tell you. He lost me for good, if I wasn't lost already.

Something must've happened one day, a violent event. My friend and I were discussing it while listening to 'The Whole of the Moon', one earbud each, and my friend acknowledged that she was terrified because of where she lived on the other half of town from where I lived. 'But you'll be okay,' she said. 'You live up among them.'

This confounded me. I didn't understand how on Earth she thought that and felt easy in confessing. Was it because she went to a Protestant primary; division first? Apart from at church, my experience had always been mingled.

In secret, *that* was always present, even here in big school, where we were juxtaposed and intertwined. It's hard to displace a vigilance inserted at the beginning. How the heck could you read Lorca and think 'up among them'? Defining oneself by negation felt so insecure, parching; you had to fend off each imagined threat. I'd rather open wide, take everything. Opening too far was better than living in a nervy paralysis, praying I alone was right. Freedom's precious when you've watched others choose not to be free. I was practical, young, harsh, and my spirit wasn't in it anymore.

My friend didn't see as I saw but didn't mean harm. Had she any mates who weren't like her, who weren't like *us* in her view? I could've talked with her; I didn't. It turned me off. I went cold, floated away. What if she didn't know then what she'd later grow to understand? What if I'd misinterpreted her, or not understood what would later surface? Not knowing isn't evil. Maybe I ought to have been more forgiving, to have paused. I feared that if I raised it, she might admit what I couldn't bear to hear. I judged her alarm, withdrew from her and anyone who maintained that affinity, that anxiety. I so ached to elude the spiteful differentiation, stretching to live a broad exciting life, to let mingle and keep flowing and include only the loving, the harm-free. Without noting a contradiction, I gave up on my friend, viewing her as a lost cause, a narrow one. I had to distance myself from them.

But I'm an heir of people who once played instruments in the marching band. To them it wasn't wrong. They didn't hate; I've asked. Not that I speak for them all. To some, the march was a festival, while the village band brought moments of togetherness, a common gesture, a link to time and ancestors, their path to music – a touch of craic. I'll go on if you remain open.

My granda-on-my-mother's-side began playing the accordion as a boy when it was donated to him by an old man in the village. Being entrusted with this beautiful instrument was a rite of passage. He grew accomplished. As well as playing in parades, he performed as part of a group at a social dance in Maghera, at the bottom of the Fair Hill. This small band consisted of two Catholics and two Protestants. Later, the accordion was passed to my inquisitive aunt, who played until international table

51

tennis took precedence. The accordion was retired. My generation of the family are not into that. There's loss there as well as gain.

By my time, these celebrations appeared hostile, provoking; the existence of one was interpreted or intended as an assault on the other. Once, in patches, there'd been a softer coexistence. My inquisitive aunt says, as children, her Catholic mates celebrated the twelfth of July and she street-partied on St Patrick's Day. These holidays were there for everybody. I've never known that. I shirk most customs.

During my childhood, there were towns for one and not for the other. I'd like to think that's altered. Until recently, an old buddy from swimming lived in Swatragh, a Catholic village. A time or two on the way to hers, I've driven in error to Gulladuff. Each is several miles out the road from Maghera. I confuse them because they feel akin. I'd assumed Gulladuff was a Protestant village. Having looked, I see that's not so.

A horse-riding pal used to live in Castledawson (half-and-half) near Knockloughrim (more Protestant, I think, I'm not sure) and Bellaghy (more Catholic), where water-skiing friends were.

A choir mate came from Ballyronan, an uneven combination of Catholic and Protestant, where there's a pretty marina on the brink of Lough Neagh. A brainy girl in English class was close to the lough in the South Derry parish of Ballinderry, mostly Catholic. Slightly further inland, you'd find Coagh, mostly Protestant, which was the village of a daunting tennis-opponent.

My biology teacher received intimidating instructions to move house because her family was the sole of that kind left in the area. This happened both ways. As kids we laughed. We laugh often. It disperses the poison, nods at absurdity.

Maghera was a fusion. The main shopping street was roughly bisected. No doubt some individuals frequented only one piece of the town, never crossing the threshold of the other. At random, we lived in both.

In the eastern half, Protestant-owned shops and bars proliferated. Ulster Bank was there, the medical centre, garden centre, the library. You'd find the Protestant primary school, a now-vanished Protestant comprehensive, the Presbyterian church and St Lurach's, the Church of Ireland. Adjacent to the new churches were the ruins of old St Lurach's. Morsels of this ancient church – a carving of the crucifixion – date back to the tenth century. According to the *Annals of Ulster*, it was ransacked the century before by seafarers, the Vikings.

In the western half, mostly Catholic-owned shops and bars were located. Here, among other properties, you'd find the chapel, the GAA club, the Catholic primary school. Well out the Tirkane Road, if you parked, wandered slightly along, hopped a stile, took a grass track up the hill, and climbed at an angle via a twisty stone-and-mud path, you'd reach the Emigrants' Cairn. From

Carntogher's summit, through wind-yanked tears or a mesh of brilliance, you might look in a circle around you at almost the whole of the North. I didn't know names. My elders would speculate which hills, vales, great and little waterways were which.

The approximate boundary between the two halves of Maghera was the intersection of Main Street with Coleraine Road, which shoots north to the coast. The Credit Union and St Patrick's College live along Coleraine Road, so too the police station and a new recreation centre. At the aforementioned crossroads, you'd find an estate agency, Walsh's Hotel, the Northern Bank, and a draper's, owned by my family and named after my granda-on-my-father's-side. He died before I was born. Still, he was instrumental in the life I occupy, as were all who came before. They passed me things. Until last year, my family inhabited the house and garden these grandparents designed and built, which lies south-west of the town centre, on Glen Road.

This beloved road of a mile and a half ripples between the chapel on Main Street and another more rural chapel, close to where Glen Road meets Glenshane Road, a dual carriageway that rushes through Glenshane mountain. I couldn't tell you the precise composition of Glen Road now or then. Various families, known and unknown, lived here and there, including schoolmates of Chinese heritage. The road accommodated the Catholic primary, two Parochial houses and St Mary's Annexe, the first-year building for the Catholic comprehensive. It was regarded as a Catholic road. We lived 'up among them'.

What I couldn't tolerate was the splitting that my friend from Spanish class accepted, apparently without a bead of doubt. Was that already how life appeared to her – static? The idea drained me. I wasn't shaped so. I felt I was spacious, energetic, light on my toes, a chameleon sometimes, fit to burst with maybes. Even with an accidental inevitable line through the centre of my awareness, both sects lived within. I was 'them' as much as 'her'. I wouldn't've known how to be otherwise.

Today, I find this state easier to hold and balance in language because I possess a term I didn't have when young. I've long been aware, without knowing how to explain, that having formed in a subtle, motley atmosphere, I embodied not one or the other but both and more. I am, have always been, adamantly *fluid*. What crisp water that is. It's a relief to almost catch it.

British Algerian **Lias Saoudi** grew up in the Republic of Ireland, Scotland and Northern Ireland, before moving on to take a Fine Art degree at the Slade School in Bloomsbury. He is best known as the front man of genre-bending iconoclasts Fat White Family and has toured all over the world. His first book is due for publication by White Rabbit Books, early 2022.

THE MID-ULSTER MALE

When I finally arrived in London, I immediately set to work mythologising the time I'd spent in Ulster. It was an effortless process. The student body at the Slade School of Art, where I'd been accepted onto the degree course at eighteen, would believe almost anything I had to tell them about the conflicted backwater from whence I'd sprung. My favourite embellishment was a description of the school run. According to me, one made their way into Cookstown High School each day in a sort of armoured bus, with great big metal grills strewn across the windows – essential given the regularity of sectarian mob violence. My description of the hostilities braved each day – just to lay claim to a basic state education – were an exact derivative of the journey undertaken by Billy Elliot's scab father across the picket line during the miners' strike. Everybody bought it. Slightly less believable were my tales of racial discrimination. I alone embodied the ethnic minority at my high school, I informed my new social circle. Other than myself it was entirely white, and entirely Protestant, the name Saoudi on the roll call was a never-ending source of ridicule. The sourest among the pupils came up with innumerable terms of derision with which to lash me. My personal favourite had been 'Sir Nigger-lot' on account of its feudal undertones, which seemed wholly appropriate somehow. This part of my story, sadly, I hadn't had to make up.

When I was twelve, my mother threw in the towel with my father. She'd grown weary of being treated like a kitchen appliance by the belligerent Algerian. She'd met a widower, an accountant from Cookstown, County Tyrone, on a railway platform in Prestwick, near where we were living at that time on the west coast of Scotland, and decided not long after to take the leap. As I was just about old enough to make the call, my parents sat me down and asked me which of them I'd like to continue living with. Would I choose to remain in Ayr, amongst all my friends, my big brother whom I looked up to like a dad, and my actual dad; or would I follow my mother to the Emerald Isle with my little brother in tow? We'd moved from Galway, in Ireland, to Ayr six years prior, long before the rot had fully seized the marriage. The west coast of Ireland was where I'd spent the first six – relatively happy – years of my childhood. Cookstown was not Galway, however. I was hazy on the details, knew nothing of the fractured politics, but on the one trip I'd taken there with my mum and soon-to-be stepfather, I'd decided that it wasn't for me. A town that amounted to little more than a squabble of pebbledash bungalows – one of which I'd have to share with a whole new set of siblings – seemed like it might prove a drain on the imagination. Even more concerning was the idea of having to start a new school. I opted for Scotland. My mother wept tears of rage. I changed my mind. Then, before I knew it, I was sat in my first class at Cookstown High, a mysterious big red hand sewn onto the chest of my blazer.

I arrived in the summer of 1998, not long after the signing of the Good Friday Agreement, and only three days before the detonation of the Omagh bomb twenty-six miles up the road. I didn't have to travel to school in an armoured bus, but machine gun wielding British Army squadrons did make their way through our cul-de-sac several times a day. On one occasion they disarmed my nine-year-old kid brother at gunpoint. He was wielding a toy pistol, which spooked them enough to assume combat formation in his honour. There were still road blocks between the small towns, at the centre of which invariably lay an enormous corrugated iron barracks. A soldier garrisoned outside the one in the centre of Cookstown trained his rifle on me the whole way up the High Street one Saturday afternoon while I was out buying CDs, I can only assume out of sheer boredom. I recall waiting for a haircut at John's barbershop on Irish Street with my mother not long after moving there. A policeman popped his head in and told everyone they'd best evacuate, there might be a device in or around the premises, then he disappeared. Me and my mum got up to leave immediately, but most of the punters and the barber carried on as normal. Bomb scare fatigue had done away with the best of their anxieties. My stepfather had himself been on the periphery of three bomb blasts, two of them in Tyrone, to which he alluded with a devilish irreverence all too familiar in folks who grew up with the worst of the Troubles. I didn't realise until years later that this town of roughly ten thousand people had been one of the worst-affected areas in the conflict. None of it made sense in my barely pubescent brain. There was nothing here but sheep, drizzle and alcoholism. People had been killing each other over what, exactly?

Just before my family split up – before finding itself cast either side of the Irish Sea – my dad decided to drive me and my brothers from Ayr to Algeria in his old Honda. The trip lasted two and a half months, and along the way we stopped in towns and cities across Europe: London, Paris, Marseille, Catania, Rome ... We spent a month living with my Berber family in Kabylia, family I'd not encountered since I was a baby. I was introduced to new relatives on a daily basis, a total alien to my roots. Much like the North of Ireland, Kabylia had been torn apart by terrorism in recent years. Just as the Irish Border came to be known as 'bandit country', so it was with the mountainous region that the Saoudi clan called home. Young ears would pick up on fragments of atrocity still taking place elsewhere in the country, despite a recently brokered peace – it was all the adults seemed to talk about. There was perhaps even less to fight over up in the Djurdjura Mountains ... sheep, sunshine, siesta: life moved at a dead pace. Yet there were men with guns and checkpoints everywhere. Why did these remote places hum with destruction and paranoia, while the major European conurbations we'd passed through spoke only of a dazzling, infinite vitality? How was it that the complexity of millions of people piled in on top of one another bore peace, while these bad lands with their smatterings of farm folk ended up being the front lines of conflict? Age eleven, it was impossible to fathom.

The years leading up to my GCSEs were the ones I found the toughest in Tyrone. After that, the more thuggish youngsters that'd been intent on making my life a misery disappeared, off to claim their own proud little portions of decay. These kids were politicised to a comical degree, their schoolbooks adorned with anatomically proficient renderings of British Bulldogs clasping Union Jacks between their teeth, the initials LVF and UVF written across every imaginable surface: ties, blazer cuffs, pencil cases, school bags and bibles. When Sinn Féin appointed Martin McGuinness as Education Secretary of Northern Ireland in 1999, the entire school ground to a halt in mass protest. It was these same patriots that led the charge. The school gates were suddenly a throng of fluttering red, white and blue; the immortal chant of 'do you want a sausage supper Bobby Sands?' rising up from the jubilant horde in occasional gusts – many a teacher appalled, many quietly keen, no doubt. I read in a book once – I've forgotten which – a line about there being nothing like receiving a beating from an unremarkable human being. I remember the line well because I parroted it for years in London when waxing lyrical about the tough times endured in the province. I now see that I was off the mark. The lads that picked on me were anything but. The high tide of Empire had rolled back out to sea, leaving behind these imperilled and stagnant little pools. They were clasping at a country that no longer existed, condemned to a crumbling narrative that could no longer make sense of itself. Hounded by the unreality of their origins, they had chosen loathing over mediocrity. It was an ugly choice, but there was nothing unremarkable about it.

I fell in love for the first time with a girl who lived at the opposite end of town, on the Monrush estate. It was a world away from the relative splendour of the cul-de-sac I called home, where Catholics and Protestants of a slightly more affluent hue lived comfortably side by side in their detached bungalows. Each of us had a little room to breathe, there were no flags, no painted curb sides, no murals. Her overcrowded neck of the woods was dominated by loyalist iconography of every kind. *Long Live King Rat!* the walls declared. To and from the local Tesco you were watched over by the balaclava-masked heroes of the struggle for continued Britishness, by paintings of curiously disembodied machine guns floating in a sea of bright orange and innumerable, shoddily proportioned red hands, beneath which you were constantly implored never to surrender. The youngsters regaled you with tall-sounding tales about the involvement of their families in the Troubles: 'My uncle Johnny crucified a taig up in Belfast!' 'My da was in the Maze for kneecapping seven Fenians!' 'My big brother and Billy Wright were like *THIS*!' Et cetera, et cetera ... It was common for most of the locals to keep little pictures of the Queen on their mantelpieces. Here at the bitter end of her Kingdom, she was everywhere. It began dawning on me just how far a little disposable income goes toward the easing of political tensions.

Even though she was my only friend in the world, I broke up with my girl. She'd started dressing a bit goth, she was a wilful outsider, like me, but I thought our being together only brought on more heat. Two freaks made twice the target. By shutting myself off and trying to avoid getting knocked about, I condemned myself to complete loneliness. I never plucked up the courage to explain to her why. Walking home from McDonald's one evening eating ice cream I'd been attacked by a gang of lads in front of her. They thumped me in the back of the head – as per usual – and called me a filthy little jew-nosed nigger. The hiding itself wasn't all that severe, as hidings go. It was my reaction to it that haunted me. I would lie awake in bed at night reliving it over and over again, inserting fantasies of heroic, retributive violence on my part one minute, and collapsing under the weight of the truth the next. My little brother had endured similarly miserable trials in the province. He dealt with it by stabbing one of his assailants with a pencil one day. He hospitalised the kid. After that, they left him alone. I simply didn't have the stomach for it. My tactic was endless bargaining. I would attempt to talk my way out. There are few greater humiliations in this life than looking back on yourself attempting to smooth things over with people who have just spat in your face. It sent me tumbling down into myself, down into a suicidal depression. It was around this period I began swapping reality for art, books, music and film. If it weren't for those things and the support of a few good teachers at the high school, I'm quite sure I would have drowned.

My mother was being stalked in Cookstown so we upped sticks and moved to Dungannon, ten miles up the road. By this time I was old enough to get a part-time job. I didn't really need the money, I needed something to do at the weekends that wasn't kicking a ball around with my little brother on the estate which neighboured our new cul-de-sac. I needed a social life. I took a position at the local meat factory, working on the lines. Toil started at the crack of dawn, and continued indefinitely, depending on the size of the supermarket order. Sometimes you'd finish at two, sometimes six. In a way, being stood there in a giant freezer, sifting through pieces of flesh, arranging them into neat little plateaux upon trays of polystyrene, then placing them onto a conveyor belt – all the while pounded by the latest Ronan Keating smash – helped thaw out my soul. I didn't make any friends at

Dungannon Meats, but what it did was show me that time could indeed stand still. That it was possible for time to collapse in on itself completely, all you needed to do was apply the right density of boredom. It's the closest I suppose I've come to a near-death experience. It was utterly confounding to me that people could do this full time, for years. A great many of the locals chose not to. Many emigrated from the small towns, searching for something more tenable, something that paid more than a fiver an hour and didn't involve the constant sound of a buzz saw slicing through bone. That's when the first black faces started showing up in town, migrant workers from East Timor that everybody referred to as the Portuguese.

The Eastvale estate where my brother and I went for a kick-about almost every afternoon was analogous to the one my girlfriend had grown up on. The same sectarian fixation and economic deprivation was evident everywhere. We'd kick the ball around with lads who lived down there until it got dark, then make our way to the garage on the outskirts of town to buy pop before heading back up the hill to our bungalow. I was a little older than that gaggle of boys. The youngest of them being around 11, the oldest maybe 15. On one such journey to buy tins of Coke and Dr Pepper after sweating it out for hours, they noticed a few of these new migrant workers – Portos they kept calling them – making their way back into town on foot from the factory, which was a couple of miles out. They immediately set about making monkey noises, screaming abuse. There was real venom on their tongues. The immigrants didn't make much of it, just tried to ignore it and continue on their way. I looked at little Stephan, the youngest of the bunch, going at it full throttle, hurling rocks at them with every bit of might he had in that little frame of his, then turning around to smirk at his pals. Me and my brother were disgusted, but not in the remotest bit surprised. Nor were we surprised ten years later to hear that Stephan and his elder brother had both been in and out of prison on drugs and violent crime charges since we left town.

One of the first things I did after leaving home, after moving to London to start life anew, was make my way back to Algeria. With a student loan in the bank, I was in a position to buy my own ticket, so me and a couple of friends from college made our way over there during the summer. On my last visit, construction had started on a small road around the back of my gran's house leading up to the village, a distance of about one mile. The best part of a decade had passed and this was still nowhere near completion. Much like where I'd just spent my adolescence, the place was in almost complete stasis. I soon found out about one significant shift in the region however, from a gaggle of young men that referred to themselves as my cousins. Everyone in that village is your cousin if your second name is Saoudi. In pidgin French they told me they'd found work as security guards on large infrastructure projects elsewhere in the country.

They explained that the government was bringing in hordes of migrant workers from China to build highways and the like. It was their job to watch over this labour force and the raw materials armed with rifles. I wondered how harsh life must be in China if a place like Kabylia held some kind of economic allure. 'Did you get on with the Chinese?' I asked them. 'Are they fitting in over here? You got Chinese food yet?' 'No!' They cackled in unison, *'Je deteste, je deteste la Chinois! Regarde Lias regarde ...'* Cousin Boubker took to his feet excitedly and pointed a finger into the middle distance, at an empty stretch of mountainscape, then clasped his arms around a machine gun made of thin air. *'Regarde la Chinois Lias Kaci, regarde* ... BANG BANG BANG BANG BANG!'

LANGUAGE

Orla McAlinden is an award-winning novelist and short story writer from Portadown, currently living in Kildare. Her Famine-era novel *The Flight of the Wren* (2018) won the Cecil Day Lewis Award. Her short story collections have won numerous prizes including the Eludia Award and the Irish Short Story of the Year award.

ANOIS TEACHT AN EARRAIGH: ULSTER PRESBYTERIANISM AND THE IRISH LANGUAGE REVIVAL(S)

Anois teacht an earraigh
Beidh an lá dúl chun síneadh,
Is tar eis na féil Bríde
Ardóidh mé mo sheol.

Irish speakers know these lines. We may not know many more, but we know these. We know them the way English people know Wordsworth's most treasured opening words. We wander lonely as a cloud, but are lucky enough to wander in two languages.

Antoine Ó Raifteiri most famous poem , 'Cill Aodáin', is on my mind this cold, wet February morning, as I discover the first brave stems of early budding daffodils near my home.

Now cometh the spring,
The days will be stretching,
And after the feast of St Bríd,
I will raise my sail.

I too long to raise my sail now that the short, cold days of winter are drawing to a close. I too wish to return to my homeplace, not the scenic, sea-swept landscapes of Ó Raifteiri's Mayo, but the rather more prosaic streets and dull semi-detached homes of Portadown, in County Armagh. There, unlike the blind bard, as Ó Raifteiri was known, I will not seek a month's refuge among childhood friends. My ambition is rather less expansive.

I just want to sit in my mother's kitchen, listening to stories I don't understand, about people and families I no longer remember, having left Portadown at eighteen without a backward glance. After we exhaust the tales *You do know them, her father's first wife was a Lavery, and they lived beside the sweet shop* ... we will pin my mother's cat to the ground, wrap him in a bath towel, and I will clip his front claws with my mother's nail clippers. My five years in veterinary college in Dublin thus justified, I will climb into my car and drive back to Kildare, to my husband and to the four children who have not seen their grandmother for a year.

Ó Raifteirí – blinded, maimed – was the only-survivor of a clan of eight children, all swept into the grave by the smallpox which robbed the poet of his sight, but not of his vision. Just like the smallpox of Ó Raifteirí's era, this new plague of our own time now has a vaccine, and I need only wait out the last few months of fretful tedium before I set eyes on my childhood home and my mother again.

Unlike Ó Raifteirí, it is not my own infirmity which keeps me from my journey, nor poverty, nor the vagaries of winter, but the limits imposed upon us all by the coronavirus, by the ineptitudes of our respective governments, by our collective inability to elect representatives who might have worked together to protect our tiny island and its tiny population from disease and death. Our island status squandered. Our bloody Border.

With such different approaches to public health on both parts of the island, would I have to run the gauntlet at the Border? Tales abounded throughout the pandemic of fines and penalties, of the Garda Síochána admonishing those who sneak across on unessential errands. I could slip like a wraith across a silent and secret road, perhaps one of those freshly reopened in recent decades. But to what avail? The registration plates of my Kildare car would mark me out for disapproval, and I have always been a coward, believing that obedience will preserve me, despite all the people I have known for whom such obedience provided no such hoped-for protection.

And if I muster the courage to cross the Border without societal consent, will I gather my mother up, fresh from her second shot-in-the-arm and drive through Edenderry, past the church of St Gobhan to eat stir-fried beef and noodles in the hotel bar at Seagoe? Or will our lives have shrunk too small even for such long-accustomed habits, take-away food available only (a fine big car park, has the Seagoe Hotel – my mother approves –

and an elderly waiter who has been flirting with her for almost forty years. So she says.)?

One thing I know I will definitely *not* do, when I finally am reunited with my mother, is start quoting Irish-language poetry at her. When my mother was born in July 1938, it was into a state which didn't celebrate our island's shared linguistic history. When she ran away from St Michael's boarding school in Lurgan in the 1950s, I'm quite sure she didn't bring any treasured Irish grammar books home with her to the small farm in Derrykeeran and the bustling family she missed so much.

After this small Northern State of ours was founded, one hundred years ago, a linguistic apartheid sprang up in a febrile sectarian atmosphere already deeply suspicious and rife with division. Partition of the countryside happened at the stroke of a pen in Downing Street. The language which had once been truly *all of ours* was partitioned into (proudly) *ours* and (dismissively) *theirs*, depending upon your background, completing a process begun hundreds of years earlier, despite the best efforts of language enthusiasts from all traditions on the island.

My father certainly didn't learn much Irish at school, if any at all, but the few phrases he had, he used inexhaustibly and cheerfully, and frequently inappropriately. My mother, in my experience, has rarely ever had a word of Irish upon her lips, not even a prayer, learned by rote in some schoolroom long ago.

When I 'got my Irish', as the phrase goes – not from my parents, but from the teachers of St Patrick's Academy, Dungannon – I lived in Portadown, on a 'mixed street', a phenomenon which seems almost to have disappeared in the decades since I left home thirty years ago. There weren't many Catholic children, but we made up for our relative scarcity with our exoticism. How jealous my friends were when I would pick up a carelessly dropped Black Jack or Fruit Salad from the ground and solemnly make the sign of the cross before popping it in my mouth; all germs extirpated by this Papist ritual. I tried to teach them the simple sign, so they too could *bless* any little treat that tumbled from their sticky paws onto the floor, but they were shy of it. How they laughed as they peeled the sticky, fragile wrappers off their Cadbury Creme Eggs, in the weeks before Easter, while I suffered the bitter and sugar-deprived indignities of Lent.

It was from these same friends that I first learned that the language I was studying in school – the language of my father's kindnesses and stumbling endearments – was a thing of shame and scorn.

'Turn off that Papist heathen gibberish,' Pamela's mother called out one day in the mid-1980s, shortly after some technological miracle had boosted the transmission signal so televisions in Portadown could start showing RTÉ for the first time. Whether we liked it or not. I liked it. Pamela's mother did not. Nor did she know that I was in her home, quietly playing with Pamela's much-envied Sindy doll's horse on the floor, hidden by the sofa.

Soap-sudsy arms akimbo, dripping down the front of her nylon pinny, she strode in from the kitchen muttering. 'First the blinkin' heathen gabblin' Nu-chat, then the dratted bongs.'

I stared at her, amazed. Not only did she not seem to understand that the *Nuacht* programme, just before tea-time, was only the news headlines spoken in Irish, and that, at 6 p.m., the bells of the Angelus – calling for a minute of reflection and prayer – could be safely ignored. More shocking was the realisation that real human adults in Pamela's house actually said *blinkin'* and *dratted* when they so obviously meant *bloody* or even worse. Protestants were weird. But not half as weird, according to Pamela's mother, as learning a language that nobody in the real world had ever heard of, and which was broadcast purely and simply to annoy the good Presbyterian folk of Portadown.

> *Fágaim le huacht é*
> *Go n-éiríonn mo chroí-se*
> *Mar a éiríonn an ghaoth*
> *Nó mar a scaipeann an ceo*

It was years before I learned the history of our shared province and the history of our once-shared language, which would have enabled me to tell Pamela and her parents of the proud and ongoing role of Ulster's Protestant – and especially Presbyterian – communities in the preservation of the Irish language.

They would not have believed me anyway, no more than her little brother had believed me when I told him that the effigy of the 'Fenian traitor' Robert Lundy he was so looking forward to burning on his Eleventh of July bonfire was neither Irish nor Catholic, but in fact a Scottish Protestant. In his view of the world, this fact could not be true. Therefore, it was not true, and I eventually stopped insisting that it was, for nothing on this earth is more stubborn than a young boy faced with a slightly older, slightly wiser, young girl.

I do solemnly declare it,
that my heart soars
when the wind rises
and disperses the fog.

Perhaps I should have tried harder to blow away that fog of prejudice and ignorance. Perhaps I could have tried to persuade Pamela and her brother of the importance of the Irish language, and the role their Presbyterian forefathers had played in its survival. Instead, Pamela's mother told me sternly, 'there'll be no Irish spoken in the townland of Clounagh' (*Cluaineach;* 'the place of the water-meadow'), before she shooed both of us back out onto the street.

When Pamela's family visited their granny in her small red-white-and-blue-kerbstoned terrace in The Annagh, and she complained of the dampness and the effect on her poor joints of living in 'Rheumatism Row', I might have pointed out that the clue was in the name. The Annagh (*Eanach*; 'the marsh') close to the floodplains of the River Bann. When they hopped into a sparkling and freshly polished car each Sabbath to drive to *Éadan Doire*, the 'hill-brow of the oak grove', to attend First Presbyterian church of Edenderry under the shadow of a giant, triumphal Orange arch, I might have reminded them of the legacy of the Irish language activist, the Reverend Doctor Henry Cooke, leader of the Presbyterian Synod of 1836.

But I didn't remind them, because I didn't know; no more than they. All I knew was, Irish was for Catholics, even if they only knew how to mumble the Hail Mary, and nothing else. Irish was not for Protestants, and they were fond of showing me. I passed my GCSE Irish exam with flying colours, put my *Foclóir Gaeilge-Béarla* on the bookcase beside my equally redundant *English-French*, and *English-German* dictionaries, and forgot all about the native language as it pertained to the geography, history and culture of the town of *Port an Dúnáin*.

The early Presbyterian community of Ireland had deep and sustained links with the Presbyterians of Scotland, the majority of whom were either Gaelic speaking or bilingual, and to them it seemed the most obvious thing in the world that they should learn the native language of their new home in Ireland. From the 1600s onwards, Presbyterians all over Ireland learned the Irish language and were among the first to set up a system of schools where Irish people learned to read and write in order to have personal access to the Bible *as Gaeilge*; one of the tenets of Presbyterianism being personal acquaintance with the Good Book.

As late as 1795 they were still advertising Irish classes in Belfast: 'By our understanding and speaking it we could the more easily and effectually communicate our sentiments and instructions to all our Country-men; and thus mutually improve and conciliate each other's affections'.

At their highpoint, Presbyterian schools numbered in the hundreds and educated tens of thousands of Irish speakers. Ireland's Presbyterians found no difficulty in accepting that they could be simultaneously Irish, British, bilingual and Protestant.

In an article written in 2015, Jim Stothers, Deputy Clerk of the Presbyterian General Assembly reminded his readers of events of 1836, when the Presbyterian Church of Scotland formally received the Presbyterian Synod of Ulster into its communion. A prominent member of the Ulster Synod, Reverend Doctor Henry Cooke – who, in modern parlance we would describe as an Irish language activist – addressed the Assembly in celebration and, 'in a speech sprinkled with Irish words and phrases', informed their Scottish visitors of the Ulster Synod's plans: to share the Good News of the gospel with those who 'speak exclusively or generally in the native Irish tongue'.

Stothers quotes Cooke's 1836 address: 'For advancing and perpetuating this part of our work, the Synod has lately enacted, "... that all her students must study the Irish language ... And [we] trust you [the Scottish delegation] may yet be spared to see the day, when on visiting the Synod of Ulster, you may adopt the tongue of your native hills in addressing us, and not be necessitated to enquire at any of us, *An labhrann tu Gaeilge?* [Do you speak Irish?] "'

In a spring 1997 *History Ireland* magazine review of Roger Blaney's 1996 book, *Presbyterians and the Irish Language*, Caoimhghin Ó Murchadha states: '[T]here were a number of congregations where Irish/Gaelic was, by far, the majority language, and that the custom of having Irish-language preaching every second Sunday in other areas also implies a substantial Irish-speaking congregation. Blaney contends that at least one-eighth of Presbyterians had been recruited from the native Irish-speaking population, that at least one quarter of the incoming Scots were Gaelic-speaking, and that another eighth of congregations used Irish both to speak to their Irish neighbours and to converse with Irish-speaking members of their own congregations. He argues that conservative estimates suggest that at least half of all the early Presbyterians in Ulster were Irish/Gaelic speakers.'

All of this, I assure you, would have come as a nasty shock to Pamela and her family. Decades after leaving Portadown, and being only vaguely aware of her good work – and pioneering social enterprise – I had the good fortune to meet Linda Ervine, Irish language activist and proud East Belfast unionist, at the Rostrevor Literary

Festival 2019. Among the many facets of her fascinating talk, the one that struck me most was her rueful reflection that every single piece of resistance, every snide comment, every accusation of 'Lundyism', betrayal or naivety that she encountered in her discovery and study of the Irish language has come from within her own Protestant community. And so, her East Belfast language centre *Turas* has set out to reclaim the truth of Belfast's bilingualism.

One of the most fascinating projects to spring from the *Turas* at the Skainos Centre on the Newtownards Road is the *Gaeilgeoirí of the Great War*; an initial exploration of the bilingual working-class men from the industrial streetscapes of East Belfast who fought for King and country in 1914-1918. The seventy-four Irish speaking soldiers featured in the research all identified themselves as bilingual in the 1911 census. They included family groups, workmates, and Catholic and Protestant neighbours who fought alongside each other in the trenches. These Irish speakers were drawn from all parts of the community, including members of East Belfast UVF and some – like William Spence of the Inniskilling Fusiliers – who had signed the Ulster Covenant in 1912. George Wright is not the stereotypical name one would associate in the modern era with fluency in the Irish language. Nor is William Polly, a bilingual member of the Strandtown Unionist Club, who died of his wounds after the Battle of the Somme. The photograph on the *Gaeilgeoirí of the Great War* project website of young Jasper Gammon – a bilingual Presbyterian – in his unform, is utterly heart-breaking in its youth and innocence. In 2021, he would be judged barely old enough for a part-time job in a super-market let alone fighting in a war. He returned from the conflict, 40 per cent disabled, according to his military pension record.

It should not have come as such a surprise to me to find out about this East Belfast Gaeltacht of 1914, for I have long known it was in Belfast that one of the first branches of *Conradh na Gaeilge* (The Gaelic League) was established. The Belfast League was formed in August 1895 on Upper Beersbridge Road, East Belfast, just two years after the national organisation had been founded in Dublin by Douglas Hyde, himself the son of a Church of Ireland rector.

A prominent unionist, Dr John St Clair Boyd, was elected president of the Belfast League, and PT McGinley, who later founded *Ardscoil Ultach*, a teacher training college which promoted the Ulster dialect of Irish, was elected vice president. One month later, in September 1895, the League held its first public meet-ing in Belfast. In a matter of just a few years, the Belfast branch of *Conradh na Gaeilge* had members as diverse as army officers, Catholic and Protestant clergy, factory workers and members and leaders of the Orange Order. Notable among the British army officers who flocked to celebrate their native language was Lieutenant-General William Porter MacArthur KCB, who rose to become director general of all medical operations in the field during the first years of the Second World War. Like many of Ulster's Presbyterians, he honoured their long tradition, *ag tógáil clainne le Gaeilge*, raising his children with Irish as their first language.

After the war, as mayhem and rebellion broke out across the land, and the hastily-drawn Border finally clamped its hand around the six counties in the north-eastern part of the island – highlighting and intensifying sectarian tensions that had never been far from the surface – the Irish, Catholic, Great War soldiers south of the Border were reviled and hid the fact of their service. In the North, the British, Protestant Great War soldiers of Northern Ireland started to suppress and gradually lose touch with their second – or in many cases first – language.

In 1922, the newly formed Department of Education in Northern Ireland removed the post of Irish language organiser, and withdrew grants previously paid to the Irish Teacher Training College for the improvement of Irish language teaching. The new Education Act of 1923 banned Irish as an optional subject in the senior school standards (classes). In 1926, it was further banned in standard 3 and 4, reducing the number of pupils studying the language by an estimated 70 per cent in the first half decade after the formation of the state. In 1933, all payment toward the teaching of the language in primary school was withdrawn and the remaining numbers of primary school pupils studying the language collapsed.

Lord Craigavon in 1936 asked, 'What use is it here in this progressive busy part of the Empire to teach our children the Irish language? Is it not leading them along a road which has no practical value ... we do not see that these boys being taught Irish would be any better citizens.'

All of this has now led to the point where a unionist politician can know so little of the language that shapes the landscape of his life that he can dismissively sneer, 'Curry my yoghurt' (*go raibh maith agat*) when addressing the Speaker of the House in the Stormont chamber; a position Pamela's mother most assuredly would have approved of, and which hopefully her great-grandchildren will reject.

In the meantime, I wait for my vaccine, and that longed-for journey home to see my mother.

Is dá mbéinnse i mo sheasamh	If I could but stand
I gceartlár mo dhaoine	in the heart-centre of my folk
D'imeodh an aois díom	the years would fall from me
Is bheinn arís óg	and I would be again young

Michelle Gallen's debut novel, *Big Girl Small Town*, was shortlisted for the Costa First Novel Award, the Comedy Women In Print award, an Irish Book Award and the Kate O'Brien Award. Short stories were her first love. She has had work published in Irish, UK and US anthologies and magazines including *Mslexia*, *The Stinging Fly*, *Cyphers*, and *QWF*.

ON THE WALL

John Smyth was a pillar of his community, a tower of strength in his local church. He was a man of good reputation among the local Order, respected for his God-fearing ways. He walked righteously through his autumn years, tending his farm, his animals and his soul as he strode. John Smyth was a man bound to the Lord and His Teachings. John Smyth was Saved.

But early one summer morning, as the barley ripened in the fields and the river ran slow under the trees, the blessed peace of John Smyth's soul was disturbed. He had stepped out of the house which his great-great-grand-father had built and walked to the crate at the end of the lane to pick up the milk, as was his tradition. When he turned around, the milk bottle dropped from his hand and shattered on the ground. Words were scrawled in red across the whitewashed wall at the front of his house. Without his glasses, John could not read the writing. He paused to pick up the broken bottle before hurrying back down the lane. When he rounded the blind corner at the turn into the yard, he saw the full extent of the desecration: large red letters spelling out *Vótáil Sinn Féin*. John Smyth had no learning in the useless Irish language, but he had a fair understanding of what the writing meant. His face burned as he strode inside the house.

Hazel Smyth stared at their front wall, wiping her dry hands on a clean blue tea-towel, shaking her head. Eventually, the couple went back inside to resume their breakfast. They discussed the incident at measured intervals during the meal, observing that although they were both light sleepers (alert to the sound of the Lord's footfall on the stair), neither of them had heard a thing. John's anger grew throughout the meal. He took no pleasure in the velvety soft-boiled egg he ate with home-cooked brown bread. His tea seemed bitter, and tasted no better after the addition of an uncustomary teaspoon of sugar. His wife stared quietly out the window until she sensed his disapproval at her idleness. She got up to clear the breakfast dishes as her husband swallowed down the last of his tepid tea. He announced that he was away in to pick up the papers, and that he'd call into Wilson's hardware for masonry paint. His car roared into town faster than usual, the hedges bouncing in the whiplash of his wake.

'Tidyin' her up for the winter, are ye John?'

John, who had long been prepared for the Everlasting Winter, was indignant at the suggestion his masonry might be slovenly, so he reluctantly explained the act of vandalism. Wilson was sympathetic and offered a discount on the paint, noting that many's another had been tried and tested under similar and worse circumstances. John assented that he was not alone in his Suffering.

Later that day, the scarlet letters of *Vótáil Sinn Féin* glowed less fiercely under a coat of Dulux masonry protector. Despite his desire to blot out the red letters as quickly as possible, John Smyth decided to wait the stipulated forty-eight hours before applying a second coat. During the day he found it almost easy to ignore the glowing letters, and he faced his house proudly. When a few neighbours called in to offer support, John glared at the words with disdain. But later that evening he found himself averting his gaze, avoiding the half-covered writing that seemed luminescent in the blue dusk.

The second day, John startled a young woman who was walking into the yard. She introduced herself as a reporter and asked if she could take a photograph of the sectarian graffiti she'd heard about. John curtly replied that he'd whitewashed his walls. But the reporter's gaze travelled to the wall behind his broad back.

'Jesus Christ! You can still see it! That'll definitely come out in a photo. Maybe you'd stand to the side? And your wife too? Do you have a wife?'

John Smyth heard only the first profanity from her sloppy mouth. From behind the net curtains, Hazel watched him race the girl off his land. When he walked back into the yard, breathless, she saw him enter the shed. He emerged with the tin of paint and a masonry brush. Although it was not the third day, John spent the afternoon methodically painting a final coat of white over the red letters, his ears cocked for the sound of a car engine, or rustling in the ditches behind him.

It was late autumn. The harvest had been brought in and God thanked for his blessings by Church and man. John deposited a tidy wee sum in the bank while Hazel lingered longer than usual in her pantry, staring into jars dark with fruit preserves and pickled vegetables; things that had once swollen and ripened the branches around the house, now suspended in syrup, steeped in vinegar. The house gleamed inside and out, and it was rare now that John thought of the letters beneath the immaculate white. He knew that by the end of winter, the words would have faded from the blank wall in his mind. John longed for winter, the purity of a heavy snowfall, the blindfold of absolute darkness, the reduced frequency of his neighbours' visits.

It was still dark when John Smyth woke to his wife's cries.

'John! Oh, John! Come down quick!'

His wife had never once woken him during the forty years of their marriage. He threw the covers from his body and climbed out of bed, ignoring the ache in his bones.

'Quick John, quick!'

'Houl' your whisht woman! I'm coming.'

Downstairs, Hazel stood staring at the half-set breakfast table, her wet eyes wide, the sugar bowl smashed at her feet on the stone floor. When John had first married Hazel, she had been a clumsy woman. But after years of patient training, John had slowed her jerky, awkward ways, creating the sluggish but deliberate woman before him who made few mistakes. This breakage of a family heirloom pained him.

'What ails ye?'

Hazel pointed to the mantelpiece where a Coronation Day photograph of Her Majesty The Queen usually hung. In its stead was a framed portrait of that brat, Bernadette Devlin.

When the police arrived later that morning, the elder constable admonished John for removing the portrait from the wall, an act that may have ruined the chance of fingerprints. As they questioned John about suspicious noises or other incidents, he saw the red letters glowing once more behind his eyes. He recounted the graffiti incident (spelling the words letter-by-letter twice over for the younger police constable). When asked by the older police constable why he had not reported the event, John stated that the police had enough to be dealing with, without wasting time on petty vandalism. The elder constable nodded his head wearily, and said sure didn't everyone have enough to be dealing with? Then he remarked that they were lucky nothing had been stolen. Hazel, deep in her pantry, flinched and stood still, waiting for John's response.

'With all due respect, Constable, I would like to remind you that there has been a theft.'

The policeman frowned and nodded, then scribbled something in his notebook.

'If it's alright with you, Mr Smyth, I'd like tae take a look around. See how these bucks got in.'

The old farm cottage, with its thick stone walls, heavy wooden door and small cautious windows had always felt safe, if not impenetrable to John. The police found no signs of forced entry, leading them to the conclusion that the trespasser had either come down the chimney unseasonably early or that the elderly couple may simply have forgotten to latch the door. Either possibility left John Smyth stony-faced. He watched the tremble in his wife's hands as she carried the tea tray to the table. He knew he'd have bother calming her down after this. He was satisfied that she had merely brought bare mugs of tea, not offering her scones or dark plum jam (John was loath to bless the police with the fruit of his well-pruned orchard). As they drank, the younger constable advised John to search his land for the missing portrait, as he reckoned the trespassers would have dumped it soon after their getaway. John nodded, seething as Bernadette Devlin glowered rebelliously at him through a clear plastic evidence bag.

Over the next few weeks, John tramped every inch of his farm, checking each ditch and field for Her Majesty. Hazel moved a faded reproduction of Turner's *The Fighting Temeraire* from the spare bedroom to cover the gap above the mantelpiece. But the print was smaller than Her Majesty's portrait, leaving a patch of bright wallpaper running around the plastic frame. John's customary seat had always faced the heat of the fireplace and the stern, yet wise face of Elizabeth II. But now he took to sitting in a new seat, moving his breakfast settings wordlessly each morning, until Hazel eventually understood what was happening and set his knife, fork, plate and cup in his new place.

Winter dug into the still, sodden land. John and Hazel rose early in the chilly black early each day, and retired to bed in the same way. But for the last few mornings, John had found a pain in his chest as he rose, an ache that diminished through the day, but burned hotter towards night. He did not talk of this pain to Hazel, considering it to be a private suffering, perhaps a calling from the Lord. Every morning he savoured the pain as he buttoned his shirt up over his long johns before pulling on a heavy sweater, tasting the pull on his arm, feeling his scalding heart. He moved around his farm more slowly, relishing the sights and sounds like a man who might never know another sunrise. His evening prayers grew longer, and during the Sunday service, his eyes remained closed long after the last Amen. He rose early one morning to a room that felt unnaturally bright. He drew the curtains and saw a fall of moonlit snow so heavy he knew he'd be kept from his daily run to the town. He and Hazel would be alone this day, and probably the next few days. His burning heart rejoiced and he dressed a little quicker than usual.

As Hazel prepared breakfast, John opened the door and stepped out into the heavy snow in his thick boots. His line lay silent under the starry sky. He set off down the lane wondering if young Andrew the milkman had made it through the snow; if their milk would be turning to ice in the cold. Snow had drifted on one side of the lane, sweeping all along the hedgerow. John walked to the left, lifting each foot higher than usual to step through the snow, his chest aching with each intake of icy air. When he got to the end of the row, he was unsurprised to find the milk crate empty. He harboured no grudge against the young man, though he knew Andrew's father had never missed a milk delivery; through the blizzards of that bad winter of 1955, right through the gun attacks of the '80s and '90s. As John turned back to face the house, the burning in his chest worsened. He staggered, then bent over, clawing at his jumper, trying to pull the wool and shirt from his skin, before falling into the deep snowdrift at the mouth of the lane, his eyes closed as if in a deep sleep.

John was gone too long, Hazel knew that. She sat still as the hot velvety softness of his boiled egg hardened and grew cold within its shell. Then she pulled her heavy winter coat around her, and stepped out of the warm farmhouse. She followed her husband's plodding foot-steps to the vanishing point at the top of the lane. Her eyes stinging from the falling snow, she saw the empty crate, and beside it, the stiff figure of John Smyth, half buried in a drift.

Later that morning, the doctor sat shivering in Hazel's kitchen, trying to get the woman to drink a cup of hot sweet tea. He did not want to think of the corpse in the Good Room next door. John Smyth, a man he had known long but not well.

'I'm guessing his heart gave out. I'd say he would've been feeling it for a while, Hazel. But he would never have been one to complain. And he's with the Good Lord Above now.'

Hazel continued to moan softly, her forehead furrowed and her eyes dry.

Doctor Kelly wished Hazel had not been there to see. But what could he do – no men around, the ambulance a good hour away? He wished he himself had not seen John's blue-cold chest, the skin waxy in the snow, and over his heart those glowing red letters that had been warm underneath his own fingertips: *Tiocfaidh ár lá*.

Mícheál McCann was born in Derry, and now lives in Belfast. His poems have appeared in journals across Ireland and the UK. A pamphlet of poems *Safe Home* was published by Green Bottle Press in 2020, and he was co-editor of *Hold Open the Door* published by UCD Press that same year. Alongside completing his first collection, he is currently at work on a collaborative publication with Kerri ní Dochartaigh for Skein Press's Solstice Series forthcoming in 2022.

██████DERRY

December 2020

With your eyes unfocused,
all these brake lights mesh
into puce lines of warning –
or sequinned, fraying reins.

The M2 gurgles in carbon
emissions. It stirs and hacks
like an unwell child; chorales
of car horns disturbing it.

This vein of the motorway
is well-trod, while across
the barrier, the road to Belfast
is quiet and dark. In echoes

of laser-eyed reptile films,
everyone is united tonight
if they're lucky, in flight.
The city winks less and less

the further we chart from it,
and like the blink we won't
realise is our last, suddenly
the ghostly light has failed.

As the outer remit of the city
passes, the pale puddles of light
from streetlamps halt, forcing
lonely cars to light the way in

whatever direction means home.
An odd phenomenon: hazard
lights a-blink from every car.
Not in trouble, but thanking

each high-speed kindness, each
slowing down, each letting him
go, just signalling, blinking.
Hello, I'm here. So are you.

With every few miles away
and every other road sign
that reads ████████derry
you recall how powerful

a black marker can be;
the erasing of language
as important as the forging.
And they call it lovely, lovely ...

How often did each car on
the hard shoulder resemble
a story; one without words?
You're one too, remember.

Each car and neon lorry cab
is lit by faulty door-lights or glints
of cigarettes that show the way.
Jesus, I'd follow anything.

Each of these cars caress the curve
of the slip-road as they pull off,
lit now by electric icicles,
like a story you regret missing.

If I've learned anything here
it's how we grasp one another
more than the angels flying
in our respective elsewheres.

I daydream about songs where
lyrics don't matter and days
where my ma laughs about my
kissing a lovely Protestant boy.

I say all this to say that I got home,
and have wasted too much time.
I'm away to show my da my waning
hairline, and how, if my breath

and luck continue, I'll officially
be the Better-Looking Twin.
He tells me to get fucked.
I sleep so well that night.

RAIN

i.m.

After Eavan Boland's 'Rain'

I was born between two places
and rain smelled differently in each.
      My mother wears a red scarf
            of mischief when she turns
and reminds me that the weather
smiles more across the Border.
      But on which side I was never sure.
            At least it falls the same, barrelling
to the island's wild grass, earth,
and holes in meadows too deep
      to measure. But it goes
            where we are afraid to ...
Grass stains, the mark of the foolish
enough to think the ground dry,
      not molten with water
            and buried aches and pains.
The sorer the soil, the greater
its desire to sup, turned up,
      always thirsting. A mouth wide
            open like weepers, like singers.

And with each harvest season passing
and the soil dredged, uprooted, opened,
   the long-buried roots, their provenance,
      come closer and closer to the morning.

THE PHARMACY

Just there for a pair of inhalers;
one blue, the other pinkish white.
They remind me of sweet peas,
two that have linked their arms.

The masked cashier steps forward
and calls *Michael?* The clock ticks
like a suspicious object behind me
and I turn to see this other man fully.

The pharmacy is empty save for Carly
Simon humming. She's probably behind a display
of perfumes, no Michael in sight ...
We seem to follow each other, missing

connections. As the employee stares
awkwardly I wonder if M. worries about his mother,
what might he say into the phone after the call,
or if he also wanted to dive from a height

into the cold tide. I hope he's alright,
that whatever ails him is treatable
with some colourful pills and soothing
ointments that consolidate a heartbeat.

I take his bag of medicine, confident
that I'll bump into him again. Maybe on a Tuesday
as the sun emerges boldly like a film star,
and under it we'd smile, stop. Say, *Hello, stranger.*

Luke Cassidy is a writer from Dundalk. His debut novel, *Iron Annie*, is published by Bloomsbury Books in Ireland and the UK, and Vintage Books in the USA and Canada.

A GOOD TURN

It was Mother's Day, see, an I was tryinta do a good turn for me ma, an her awful failed since I been back home. Sure I know rightly it was cause'a me, up all hours like an eejit the way I do be. She needs her sleep for her health to be good, I know rightly. Tryinta mend me ways so I was, I didn go lookin for them lads. Here's how it happened.

Cold aul day, with one'a them winds that'd cut right through you. Crisp, like a razor, an just as bright. Firm underfoot with a high enough sun for the season that was in it, though, this lingerin prickofa winter. I'd been up the night before, all through the night, as per, y'know, me, fuckin up all hours I am. The age'a me. Fuckin does me ma's head in, an mine too. Truly it does. Not my choice, not really. Rattlin round, she calls it, bangin doors an makin noise an keepin her awake too an her *needin* her sleep, sure I know that. It's what's keepin me up sometimes, the thought that it's me keepin her up, even though I try to close them doors quiet, I do. I try.

That night, I stayed up watchin them videos. Videos that teach ye bowt sleepin or what it's bowt, the science bit. But explained nice, by this English fella with floppy hair. Nice voice for an Englishman, a dead educated voice, but not like,

like the way a lot'a educated people talk, the way they do be sneerin at ye for not knowin what they do. Naw, he wasn like that. He had this nice soft way bowt him, probably cause he knew howta get a daecent sleep an that. He was tryin, really tryinta help ye figure out the whole sleepin bit.

See it was him who said that sunlight was dead important for sleep. Mad, innit? But he says that it's important to get out ta fuck an look at the sun, ta let it inta yer eyes an that, the way that yer brain knows what time is day an what time is night, cause that's dead hard these days, the screens n'all. It's called *melatonin* an ye get it from the sun, but in through yer eyes. At least I think that's the job. Mad craic altogether.

So out I go for the walk like – an here's me juss givin *a truthful statement of fact* like yis tauld me to do, but that's the only reason I was on the back road'a Mulligan's farm that day – normally I'd never go that way. I was chasin the sun, followin after it, juss walkin wherever I could still get it in me eyes. An I hadta keep walkin, cause remember, this was a chill wintery cuntofa sun we're dealin with here, not some August honeysuckle job.

Findin meself down that way, where I'd normally not be these days, I saysta meself, sure I'll call on aul Steevy Mulligan – see if he's still doin the logs an that. Cause I saw rightly that Mam's supply was runnin thin. An her too proudta say nathin, norta ask for help. She'd go without herselfta keep the house warm for me. I was only tryinta help sure.

Steevy opens the doorta me, a big heavy clunky lumber door itself, ill-fit an draughty. Steevy, the grey on him, all over him an in him, he stands there blinkin. See, he has the sun right in his eyes then an by the look'a him it's a fair while since he's had a daecent dose'a it himself.

'It's important not ta close yer eyes, Steevy lad,' I saysta him. 'An don't go reachin for yer sunglasses either!'

'What? Is that you, Paudy? Catherine's young lad?'

'Aye. Juss you keep them blinkers open, Steevy,' I says, steppin asideta make sure I'm not blockin the light from his eyes.

'The fuck're ye shite'n on bowt?'

'The melatonin. Ye need it. Gets in through yer eyes. From the sunlight. Open wide there Steevy, or ye'll not get a good night's sleep.'

'A good night's sleep?'

'Aye. I've been studying up bowt sleepin. On th'internet an that.'

'You've gone an fuckin lost it, lad. Fuck away off from here an don't be pesterin me. I know rightly it's work yer after bai, an after that time ye killed the bullock there's none round here'd trust ye behind the wheelofa tractor. Do us all a favour an fuck away off would ye?'

See, now that's the typical kindofa measley-mouthed meanness that does be in the ones round our way. One fuckin accident'll follow ye round like a bad smell, an me havin them costs well paid this years gone by. Cunts bai, they juss won't let ye let go'a it, juss keep draggin ye down inta their misery.

107

Probably cause the lot'a them don't get enough sleep. That'd explain them bein such a bunch'a grumpy pricks.

Still. I've been years workin on my self-development since then. The sleep thing was juss the latest like. I'd been doin all kindsa online courses before then. Ye haveta be the bigger person in these kinda situations, y'know. So I grit my teeth an stretched a smile across them an said, thinly, but calmly, *no*.

'No, Mr Mulligan, I'm not here askin after work. I'm not in need of work presently.'

The fuckin cheeks achin on me haigh.

'I'm here to *inquire*, as it were, if ye're still sellin the logs the way you used to.'

His face lights up an I can see fivers an tenners flashin in his eyes.

'Ach, Paudy, I'm sorry lad. Ye've juss got me at a bad time there, son, I'm not in the best'a form. I think it's this weather.'

I grit them teeth again.

'It's hardly the weather, Mr Mulligan, it'd be the melatonin. Yer in fierce want'a melatonin, I can see it by ye.'

His jaw hangs a bit slack there for a bit.

'So is it logs yer wantin? Below at yer mam's, is it? It'll be a hundred for the load, twenty for the delivery. Sterling, now. They're good dry logs, well-seasoned in the back shed there.'

'That sounds fine, Mr Mulligan. Do you have an email address?'

'The fuck would ye be wantin an email address for, lad, I'll juss throw them down to ye, an you pay me in cash. There in me claw. No messin now, I've no patience for it.'

'For the video, Mr Mulligan. For the sleepin.'

The head on him.

Anyway, I get his email off'a him, an every intention I had too, to send him them videos. Th'only way to make somethin happen is by bein the change ye want to see. If the humpy prick'd even watch them's another question. But I lost the bit'a paper he wrote it on, in the bushes I think.

Now, normally I'd'a gone back the way I came too, but see the way the sun was slopin down, I hadta change tackta follow it. I'd gotten cold stood there talkinta yon sour prick so I hastened up my pace. I wanted to be back to the bog road before sunset so I could get the last good dose'a sunlight down me.

That's how I found meself beatin cross the briars an the bushes – all overgrown that path is. I remembered it from when I was a wee lad but. So with a stick in me hand I went bowt bate'n the bushes down so I could walk by. I think it was bowt *then* that I started singin – y'know, juss to keep the cheer. Positive mental attitude n'all that. Hard to come by on the day that was in it haigh.

I wasn watchin out for bein spotted, see. I was singin out, bate'n them bushes so I s'pose I was makin lots'a noise, but they should'a seen I was only out on a walk an left me be.

Fuckin cunts bai. I didn see fuck all'a what they were doin an that's the god's honest truth, cause sure wasn I starin at the sun? But would they believe that? Not fuckin likely.

By the time I heard them, they were already on top'a me – the three'a them – and the biggest'a them landed a thump on me. Landed me in the bushes like a bag'a Mulligan's dirty wet logs.

Battered the shite out'a me, aye. Bring me for an x-ray an I'd say ye'd still find two or three cracked ribs haigh. It was that kindofa bate'n where ye stop feelin the thumps landin, they're juss like splashes'a water an yer already wet. Juss ever so often, there'd be this clickin noise, there at the centre'a me – metal soundin – an me feelin farther away from meself with every punch.

Next thing I know, they had the hands tied behind me back. The big lad, an aul buck, big scar across his eyebrow – ye probably know the cunt – he stands there, sorta squintin at me. Th'other two, sure I know them rightly. One lad, the thick lad, he was from Blaney if I remember rightly, and th'other fella, sure we went ta school together.

'You're after seein somethin you best not have, buck, An that's too bad for you. Your unlucky day I'd say,' says the big lad, the aul lad.

'I seen fuckin nathin so I didn. I was juss out for a walk.'

'For a walk? Sure no one goes walkin down this way. Who tauld ye we'd be here? Fuckin spit it bai, or yer goin in the ground, right here.'

'I tauld ye, no one. I was juss out, tryinta do a good turn.'

'A good turn, is it? Who the fuck for?'

'For me ma,' I say, more of a whimper really.

I'm already buckled over, by the laughter'a them, when scar-face-cunt gives me another dig in the gut. I feel somethin move, not where it should. Right inside me.

Dimly, I'm aware that the sun is settin behind this cunt, an him there bellowin at me. Words barely registerin, it's juss noise pourin out'a him. I'm starin past him at the fadin light – the sound'a him pilin up round me. An I'm brought back to th'accident, that day when I hit the bullock with the tractor, pinned its head agin the wall. I hadn thought'a that in years, but there it was again – that noise, the sheer white noise'a brutal, stupid pain. Bellowin from somewhere beyond himself, both that bullock an this buck roarin here in front'a me. An y'know what? In that moment I felt real pity for him, an him makin shite'a me sure. All I can see is him, castrated, confused, bleedin out from its neck an me at the wheel. The poor wee cratur, like. Never did nathinta harm no one.

LANDSCAPE

Maureen Boyle won the Strokestown Poetry Competition, the Ireland Chair of Poetry bursary and its Travel Award, and the Fish Short Memoir Prize. Her debut collection, *The Work of a Winter* (Arlen House, 2018) was shortlisted for the Strong Shine Award and her poem 'First Time' is a winner in the 2021 Fish Poetry Prize.

from INCUNABULA

VII

Summer started with the smell of a new book
bought in Bundoran in a huckster shop
full of wondrous things, like the stall of a relic seller
in a medieval market. We were staying in a big pink
pebble-dashed house in the West End, where Mrs Brady
sang in pubs, and the floors of the house were red
linoleum; the beds with iron steads high like boats floating
on a red sea. My book was Blyton, and a cold wet July
in Ireland was dull compared to a leafy green English
seaside town. I vowed to have a midnight feast
and smuggled food from all our meals, hiding it
under the iron bed so that by the feast's time
it was a feast of congealed rice and cold potato
– hardly lashings of ginger beer. And then
one night my mother bled a baby
with blood as vivid as the liverish floor.
I did not know it then but thought of it years later when,
at Midnight Mass, a woman in the seat before us rose
and left just such a miraculous mess
on the gleaming oak of the church bench.

VIII

We would go to another country over the 'Camel's Hump',
the army asking us what was the purpose of our visit,
the white-shirted customs men taking so long
that there was time to buy ice-cream cones in the queue.
That is where the milkman died
when he tried to climb the mountain,
my father would say, ritually, as we passed
through The Gap on the way to the sea.
And always, I saw the milkman in his uniform
scrambling over heather with six bottles in a holder,
losing his footing. The spilling milk becomes the frothy falls
we passed. Barnesmore was a Western pass
that might be closed by snow in winter,
or where you might see Indians lining up on a ridge
ready to charge. I would pass the time singing pop songs
loud in the back – sometimes stumbling over lyrics that
felt risqué –
The Father, Son and the Holy Ghost,
they caught the last train for the coast.
The Gap was our gateway into Donegal and safely through,
a new vigilance began – to be the first to see the sea.

IX

Rosnowlagh was a woman's place – the men coming
only on weekends with groceries ordered
from the payphone near the shop.
You couldn't buy the food in Donegal, where,
my mother said, they charged for turnips by the pound.
The caravan was cosy in the rain but we'd to chew
gum energetically to plug the condensation vents
around the windows; the gas mantles spluttering cosily
as the rain bounced off the tin roof and the waves
pounded in the background. On good evenings
the women and the wains set off on their own pilgrimage
across the beach and up the hill to the friary, passing
the big rock that marked the boundary of the lands
of the Four Masters, and which showed a gold-leafed monk
writing with a feather. The reward at the end, sweets
in Hursts' shop – the chocolate and crisps better
than at home. On some nights, all the children
would be rounded up for a midnight swim – Mrs Mc Carron
a kind of pied piper luring us to the shore with her Kerry Blue,
the waves visible only when the moon caught their
      white froth.

X

Summer ended in reverse ritual like a film rewound:
the last glimpse of the sea, chips eaten
in the car park of the chapel in Donegal Town –
my mother dividing up the fish and chips between us
so that wealth and adulthood came to be the dream
of having a whole bag all to yourself.
Then the journey through The Gap and the question,
Is that the mountain where the milkman fell Daddy?
Then the customs post, the army checkpoint and our own
house grown strange and new from our long absence:
the garden seeded and ripe, the rooms impossibly large,
tans bright in the mirrors, piles of washing,
cotton sleeping bags that smelled of the beach
to be hibernated for winter, left in the van
they'd dampen and mildew. The scroll of summer,
the back of an old roll of wallpaper, on which I'd charted
ambitions for the long unformed open weeks of days,
could now be rolled up as time was parsed again into the
     routine
of days and hours and minutes and we'd relearn the geography
of this older place: the house, the fields, the river.

from STRABANE

2

Strabane is in a pocket of mountains –
the River Mourne fed by the Sperrins –
Knocavoe, Bellcoo, Bessie Bell, Croghan;
names flowing down into the town
for housing estates and parks.

To the west the River Finn flows into it
at Lifford; its waters from the high hills
of Donegal–The Gap at Barnesmore
which feeds the flow of river water,
and of people,

come in streams from Gweedore, Glenties,
Crolley, bringing the old language with them,
and the *uaigneas* – the loneliness
of standing in this square to be hired –

most only children – sleeping in barns
and working for rich farmers.
Many would stay and make their lives here,
my father's family from the island of Arranmore.

3

Along the river, and in Donegal,
people grew flax in their fields –
the little blue flower growing well
in the river's wet beds that would rot and ret it for linen.

First, they worked in their homes
and then the Herdmans came
to build a mill and a village –
a model English village beside an Irish town.

My grandfather worked in the mill.
My mother vowed she never would,
seeing the sinister snow of scutched flax
that hid her father when she was sent
to bring him his lunch,
making him wheeze
at night when he came home,
going out into the yard and burning
a circle of white powder
which he'd breathe into his beleaguered lungs
to try and clear them –
one snow swapped for another –
a bowl by his bed to collect
the poison he'd cough up in the night.

Byssinosis, the price the workers paid
for the privilege of a wage and a tiny street house.

7

A counter-current flowed above the river at Lifford
where the Mourne meets the Finn to form the Foyle.
Under the bridge, salmon, trout, herons, kingfishers;
above, for years, miraculous cargoes
carried in pockets, bags, knickers and prams –
an argosy of all that was rationed in the North
but available down South:
chocolates, butter, sugar and shoes.
All you could wish for. My mother's pale buckskinned
Confirmation pumps ordered in Dooher's shop in Lifford,
sent from Dublin, then collected by her father
and smuggled across.

Garrett Carr travelled Ireland's Border creating maps that have been exhibited widely. His book, *The Rule of the Land: Walking Ireland's Border* was published by Faber & Faber in 2017 and was a BBC Radio 4 Book of the Week. He is a Senior Lecturer in Creative Writing at Queen's University, Belfast.

NORTH SOUTH EAST WEST

I decide to ease myself into Larne, parking my car a
couple of miles north of the town and walking from
there. My route is via a tunnel blasted through rock in the
nineteenth century. When I emerge from the tunnel, I see
a ferry on its way to Larne as well, coming from Scotland.
The vessel is about 500 feet long, blue and white, the
colours dulled by this morning's rain. Grey water peels
from the bow soundlessly. I walk parallel with the vessel
for a while before it gets ahead.

The ferry is crossing the Irish Sea from one part of the United Kingdom to another, yet its cargo will have to satisfy inspections in Larne before being allowed onwards. That's because a new customs Border is now operating along this coast. It is often called a sea Border, although in fact its rules are applied at the ports. Since the UK left the European Union such inspections have to happen somewhere. The other possible location was sixty miles away on the land Border between Northern Ireland and the rest of the island, but early in the negotiations it was decided to leave that Border open. It has seen enough trouble. I know Ireland's land Border well, have visited its towns many times. Although trucks can rumble through its towns without stopping, they are still Border towns in almost every other meaningful way. Customs inspections, however, are now happening here on the coast, and this has got me wondering: Is Larne now a Border town? I've come to find out.

The Irish Sea is on my port side and the cliffs starboard as I walk towards the town. Larne certainly has Border geography, the sea is an obvious natural frontier – more imposing than anything on the land Border – but where some people see a divide, others see an east-west link. Ferries move back and forth in a constant relay. Squeezed between the road and the steep banks are bungalows with huge windows, framing as much horizon as possible. I pass a parking bay where people can sit in their cars and gaze towards Scotland. On a good day they would be able to see it, but this morning there is nothing but a curtain of rain. A few people are parked here anyway, alone or with a silent teenager in the passenger seat scrolling through a phone.

Beneath the road is a strip of rocky beach, laid down in the Jurassic period when the sea here was busy with ammonites. I decide to walk along the beach and I'm taken by pieces of redbrick, rather than fossils, lying among the pebbles – scores of them. Although their edges are softened by the sea, many still have core-holes through them and wouldn't be mistaken for natural stone. Many have no holes and have been broken up and worn into egg-shapes, but still their gritty texture and distinct colour marks them out as oven-baked. I'm sure some of these pieces have been getting washed in and out for a century. Rubble dumping, sinking cargo, houses falling into the sea – one way or another thousands of these bricks made it into these waters and together they speak of the long-standing industrialisation of this coast.

A concrete walkway with steel railings continues along the shore into Larne. There are benches on wrought-iron legs; modern, angular and austere. A town park is at the top of the cliff and I can see a lone man standing in the bandstand up there, staring east. A few minutes later I find the path blocked by a large wire grill and a sign saying, 'DANGER Path closed due to rock fall'. I'm unwilling to accept this restriction on my movements and I'm not the first either; a lower corner of the grill has been bent back. I look around and go through. It's then that I feel I've arrived in Larne.

Even if you could ignore custom posts, towns along Ireland's land Border often found ways to let any visitor know their political allegiance, or at least the allegiance of most people on the town council. Take for example the War of Independence memorial in the Donegal Border village of Pettigo. It was carved and erected in memory of the men who died fighting British troops in the area in 1922. The stone soldier, with his stone gun, faces straight down the road that carries any traveller over the Border from Northern Ireland. It makes one thing clear: you're somewhere else now, it says, you've crossed into *our* territory. An equivalent in Larne might be the twenty-six-foot tall crown in the middle of a busy roundabout on the way into the town, erected to celebrate Queen Elizabeth's diamond jubilee and by extension the union with Britain. Larne council put up the crown without planning permission, saying it was only for the short-term. Made cheaply of thin steel, the crown looks temporary but has somehow remained for ten years. But who am I to judge, it's got a few good reviews on the internet. It seems one man brought his kids to look at it, not once but regularly. 'A great day out for all the family,' he says.

The Victorian style lamppost I find further along Larne's shore path is another marker of loyalty. The lamp is on a plinth and demands to be approached. The plaque explains that in 1914 this very lamp guided a ship into Larne carrying weapons for the Ulster Volunteer Force, who'd been formed to defend the union with Britain. The lamp is an even better match with the Pettigo memorial since they both emerged from the same phase of assertion and violence. One carved from stone, insisting that hard earth is the primary element of a nation, the other a point of light, insisting on the validity of a sea connection.

I step away from the lamp and walk back to the shore. Gulls hover in the wind, beating their wings hard and fast in order to stay in the same place. The ferry has docked and I can see its stern. I want to get around to the bow but the entire harbour zone is fenced off, so I will have to walk a wide route around the perimeter.

Through the wires I can see an expanse of concrete as big as a runway, where dozens of truck trailers await collection. From the air, I imagine the trailers create the impression of a parquet floor. Beyond the trailers I can see two harbour staff in high-visibility jackets moving back and forth between sheds. Above their heads is a 300-foot long walkway, elevated and covered. This is how passengers without vehicles board the ferries. There is nothing without purpose in the harbour zone, and not a blade of grass. Security huts, cranes, fuel tanks, massive parking bays, uniformed staff – it's all one mile-wide machine. A dual carriageway bypasses the town to link with the harbour, via what might be the biggest roundabout in Ireland. It has to be big, it mostly serves trucks.

Shortly before my visit, Larne's mayor – arguing against having customs operations here – said the town was a 'gateway to the mainland'. I think he was undermining his own point because a gate can be a site of control; a gap everything must pass through becomes a useful place to hold inspections. Ireland's land Border, on the other hand, is more like a sieve. Surely if we must have a customs operation somewhere then here makes sense. Put it inside the fence alongside all this pre-existing infrastructure, in this zone built for regulation and process.

This argument does not consider Northern Ireland's emotional compass. We're familiar with Orange and Green, Unionist and Nationalist, but there are other poles of attraction. Since it became clear Ireland would be getting a customs Border again I've heard a certain emphasis on the phrases 'North-South' and 'East-West'. They are not new terms but they seem to have gained new importance recently, become new foci of loyalty. Nationalism has supported years of initiatives leading to more North-South connection in Ireland, helping to bring about six North-South bodies and a North-South Ministerial Council. Unionist ministers have often preferred to miss those meetings, taking more interest in the East-West body that was created as counterbalance. During 2021 debates in the Stormont parliament, nationalists claimed North-South trade is more valuable to Northern Ireland than East-West trade; they had the figures. Unionists claimed the opposite and they had figures too. It looks like figures can be found for any occasion and that both North-South and East-West orientations are actually instinctual, emotional. After the Border inspections began in Larne, a unionist politician, Gordon Lyons, rang the Secretary of State asking, 'How would you feel if a Border had been put between Cornwall and the rest of the United Kingdom?' *Feel.* Lyons's feelings were running so high he ordered that work be stopped on new inspection facilities under construction in Larne's harbour zone. It is not clear if he was entitled to give this order, but it was certainly a great way to express his feelings.

Emotional compasses are the reason some of us are sure to be in favour of a North-South bridge proposed for Carlingford Lough. An economic case barely needs to be made. The same people who dismiss that idea instead call for an East-West tunnel connecting Northern Ireland and Scotland. The proposed tunnel would start in Larne. Prime Minister Boris Johnson talks about the tunnel occasionally – he understands the appeal the idea holds for some. It is unlikely that the tunnel will be built, but that doesn't matter. The proposal's improbability may actually help it do its primary job; expressing Johnson's emotional connection with Northern Ireland's East-Westerners. The Prime Minister is saying that he understands the East-West longing, and that he has those feelings too. I'm not so sure about his sincerity, but in Northern Ireland both orientations are rooted in genuine longing and they are the reason the mere symbolism of Border controls, whether on sea or land, is fraught.

I walk a couple of residential streets leading to the harbour gates. Squalls of rain pass over and parked cars shudder in the wind. No one is walking apart from me and a postwoman in a hi-vis jacket. We wave to each other across the street. Twice a police car goes by. Lots of placards have been cable-tied to streetlights; 'Larne Says No Irish Sea Border', 'No Internal UK Border'. I do not see any of these signs in the windows of homes, and not because the people of Larne are against signs in windows; there are many in support of the National Health Service. But all the anti-sea-Border signs are on fences or streetlights, attributable to no one in particular.

I know the security guards won't let me into the harbour – I don't even ask – but from near the gates I can see the ferry with its bow door open and trucks emerging. There are no delays; the trucks are down the ramp, out the gate, on the huge roundabout and away in twenty seconds. Despite the fence, I take a photograph. I take it quickly, as newspapers have reported a fear that customs staff in Larne are being observed. Threatening graffiti was sprayed on a wall near the harbour recently; 'ALL BORDER POST STAFF ARE TARGETS'. In this atmosphere I find the dark windows of the buildings across the street have a certain menace. As soon as I've taken the photo a man in a hi-vis jacket crosses the road to speak to me. He might be security, or perhaps a pro-active administrator who happened to be outside his office when I stopped.

'Just wondering what you're doing,' he says.

'I'm writing about Larne,' I say. 'I don't really need the photo, I can delete it.'

He says there's no need.

'Have the new inspections caused delays?' I ask.

'No, we're operating a light-touch and had no tail-backs so far. We've had no send-backs either, although there will have been a few send-backs on the Scottish side.'

'I'm trying to figure something out,' I say. 'If there's a Border here does that make Larne a Border town?'

He gets a laugh out of that. 'Any conclusions?' he asks.

'I got nervous before taking that photo, reminding me of how some towns on the land Border used to be.'

'Ah, yes,' he says. 'You can't take a photograph here either without a man in a hi-vis jacket approaching you.'

I tell him I agree, though really it's the men not in hi-vis jackets who are the worry. During my walk around the harbour perimeter I've developed friendly feelings towards people in hi-vis jackets. Maybe it's partly COVID and how it's highlighted essential workers, but mostly it's due to the threats daubed on walls. Threats make you choose a side and I find myself on the side of people in hi-vis jackets. I've seen many of them today through the fence, always in the middle distance, checking moorings, examining their clipboards, operating the machine.

'If we stop working, the country starves,' he says to me.

The last place I go is the wall where the graffiti was painted. It overlooks the roundabout directly outside the harbour gates. The words were pressure-hosed away a couple of days ago, leaving a pale rectangle twenty feet long, but someone returned just last night and spray-painted a cross and circle on the same wall; the representation of a rifle's crosshairs, of someone wanting to shoot you. The last time I saw this symbol was on the land Border five years ago, painted on the door of an abandoned farmhouse to scare people off buying it. The trucks roll by and I suppose some of the drivers notice the graffiti. What would a driver from England or France make of it? The symbol makes one thing clear: you're somewhere else now, it says, you've crossed into *our* territory. I look at the crosshairs a while, then the trucks, then the crosshairs again. I wonder who painted the message. By making these marks they have done more than anyone to make Larne feel like a Border town.

Dean Fee has been published in *The Stinging Fly, The Dublin Review* and *The Tangerine.* He is working on a collection of stories.

BORDER BARS

During the Troubles, Dundalk was often referred to as El Paso due to its similarities with the famous Mexican Border city. It was a town where the hard men of the republican movement stayed and waited for their next foray across the Border. They gathered and plotted in republican pubs or in old country shebeens and never really left. One of Dundalk's most notorious bars was one of my Dad's regulars, The Diamond Inn. Two interesting things happened there: I had my first ever pint there at fourteen, and a man was shot in the face with a shotgun and survived. The former was fully against my mother's wishes but I was staying with my Dad and he was much more lenient. The latter was a man released from a murder charge under the Good Friday Agreement who got into a row with a local builder and thought getting a shotgun was the way to solve it.

My older brother Mark and I lived in Cavan with our mother who stressed and strained herself working long shifts in a shower factory. My Dad lived in Dundalk and worked as a carpenter. I couldn't tell you the exact year my parents split up because I was very young when it happened, and also there was the issue of distinction. In Ireland in the 1990s you had to be legally separated and living apart for four years before you could get divorced, so for a long time we navigated the murky waters of Separation; a state close to Divorced but far enough away that there was always the hope, no matter how ridiculous, of a reunion. Other distinctions came later. Ones like *broken home*, or *single-parent family*; distinctions that had a nominative effect and would lead my teachers, when I acted up, to ask, 'Is everything all right at home?'

We didn't really talk about Northern Ireland growing up in Cavan. You'd see the odd 'IRA' scrawled on a wall or someone would chant 'Ooh! Ah! Up the Ra!', but not much else other than that. For a long time I wasn't even sure if the IRA was a good or a bad thing. When the adults around me did speak of it, it was in a low hush of confusing acronyms and softly shaken heads. A lot of *Ach sures* and *Whatcanyoudos*. Resignation and acceptance – as long as the trouble didn't come much closer. I still find it strange to think of Cavan as a Border county. Maybe it's because my hometown, Bailieborough, is located so far from the Border, or maybe my mother just wanted to shelter me from the violence of it all. The more likely story is that not many people cared. They sat on the outskirts of the unrest and kept their heads down, hoping it would blow over, praying for the unlikely day of a reunion.

It was only in my late teens and early twenties that I began to spend time in the North. Like my older brother before me, I went to live and work with Dad in Dundalk, where the job meant we spent a lot of time across the Border. On any trip up north he would note the point where Ireland became Northern Ireland, and I was always disappointed not to see an actual line. Instead, I saw fields and hills dotted with houses, nothing marked, all lacking any discernible difference from one side to the other. Later, I'd see the grey stretch of the M1 as it cut through the same fields and hoped this new connection might solidify.

I was to learn my trade as a carpenter because it was always good to have a trade to fall back on. Not that I was discouraged in pursuing the many creative endeavours I had in mind, but it was generally thought a back-up plan wouldn't go amiss. We worked on homes and building sites on either side of the Border, mixing with men with strong accents and funny ways of saying things. Funny *spakes* as my Dad would say. A lot of them were family: uncles and cousins plying the trade that was passed down to them like my Dad was trying to pass carpentry onto me. But there were others too, chancers and wheeler-dealers, foremen with big blocky mobile phones who operated in the opportunistic divide of the Border; half of them nick-named Del Boy. They *snoolyed* (another of my Dad's own spakes) around the roads with green diesel in their vans and spent tax disks in their windscreens, their eyes peeled for flashing blue lights and the nearest left turn that could take them onto backroads and the safety of the warren.

*

I spent the turn of the millennium in a small barn in County Armagh that my father jokingly called 'the Millennium Dome'. There was sawdust laid down and fairy lights hung up and adults milling around icy buckets with dripping beer bottles clutched in their hands. I was eleven years old and had no clue what the real Millennium Dome was, never mind its humble namesake here. What I knew of the millennium itself, and what might happen at midnight – if I could stay awake that long – was a general fear that the world would end. I had heard snippets of some adult conversations about planes falling out of the sky and something about a bug, but not much of it made sense to me. I was wholly consumed by the Pokémon game I had bought with my Confirmation money earlier in the year and paid little attention to what was happening around me.

The barn belonged to my auntie, my Dad's sister, Margaret, and it was here I got my first glimpse of the ignoble men who inhabited the grey, no man's land either side of the Border. One man, who would later be arrested for membership of the RIRA, told me in detail the best way to fuck a sheep. He discredited the folklorish method of putting their back legs inside your wellies, insisting instead to lie them on their backs. That way they can't get away. He told me it was like making love to a woman with a woolly jumper on, you could even give her a kiss if you wanted. On the phone to my Dad twenty-one years later I was reminded that the man had also asked me for a kiss.

Going from Bailieborough to Dundalk always felt a little illicit. We'd be promised early in the week that Dad was coming to take us for the weekend and we'd get so excited we'd sit in the window and watch for his van all day. He always drove a big Hi Ace van, replacing them every five or six years, and whether it was rusty reddish pink or completely white but for the caked dirt, the sight of it lumbering down the road towards us was always a joy. He'd step out of the driver's side in a cloud of smoke, cigarette hanging on his lip, and with a big grin on his face he'd give us a tight hug and a wet kiss in the ear. While we opened the sliding side door and threw our bags in, he and Mam would have a short chat in the garden. She'd usually ask for help with money and he'd usually upset her by saying he didn't have anything even for himself. I hated the tension between them, the bristling anger, and would just hope to go either side of it. We'd go off guiltily with Dad or simply cancel the whole thing and we'll stay with Mam. I couldn't stand being in the middle of it. When we returned on the Sunday after a weekend spinning around the country – Mark and I perched on the couch seat of the van – we'd tell Mam we had a great time and that nothing much happened. We'd say nothing about spending the day in the pub, or about the mad men who talked to us in drunken slurs and told us the various ways to fuck a sheep.

I've met these men on building sites and at parties, but it really is pubs where they shine. Dundalk's pubs were absolutely full of them, wayward souls lingering on the threshold of a war they'll never give up on — at least not idealistically. I've come to believe that they formed some of my sensibilities, especially when it comes to writing. They were walking characters, larger than life men who, for better or worse, you couldn't keep your eyes off. As I grew into myself and started joining my Dad for Friday and Saturday night pints, he would nudge my elbow and jerk his chin towards someone he thought I might find entertaining. He'd give me a quick back story and we'd go about watching whoever it was. Most of the time they'd come over and talk to us, and Dad — knowing I harboured ambitions of being a writer — would tell me to keep note of these men; that they'd make good fodder for a story. I used to slag my Dad over his rare ability to pull these people into his orbit. His openness to their nonsense seemed to magnetise them to him.

One of these characters was a man known as Crying Ollie, who clutched my hand in a dark Dundalk pub and wept when he found out that I was my father's son. He was obviously an alcoholic and had lost whatever grip he once had on his emotions, but at the time, the fact that he belied his nickname seconds after I met him was gold to me. Dad and I once did a job for Crying Ollie's brother out by the sea; a strange job where work would suddenly stop due to lack of materials, only to be restarted again weeks later when a sudden influx of old Bangor blue slates would turn up, half of which were too warped to use.

It was on this job that Crying Ollie's brother – let's call him Dave, since Ollie is not the other man's real name either – told us a story about how he had gouged a man's eyes out with his bare hands. In his glee at relaying the story he came up behind me where I was sitting pinching a teabag out of my mug, and demonstrated exactly how he did it. The hard points of his fingertips pressing on my eyes sent a pulsing impression of my own corneas back across my darkened vision.

Dave lived offsite in a mobile home propped up on breeze blocks, and his other brother – the non-crying one – lived in the old house opposite. The two men hated each other for some reason and it wasn't unusual for us to watch their shouting matches from up on the roof of the new house. We'd pause in the unrolling of a sheet of felt and, balancing on the open rafters and delicate lathes that stretched across them, we'd crouch behind the roof's peak to listen. From this height their verbal salvos got lost on the wind so it often seemed like their voices broke with emotion. The sound of their fury, cut off, gave the air a fractured texture that Dad would sense and then tell me to get back to work before we were seen to be listening. I'd return to aligning the lathes and nailing them over the felt, but my ears would remain cocked for drama.

The real drama came unexpectedly one Sunday when I was returning by train to Dundalk from a weekend in Dublin. Dad called me and asked if I had seen the news. My old friend – as Dad referred to Dave – had killed his brother. The brother had been drinking in town and had worked himself up into a rage. He gathered a couple of off-colour friends and the three of them attacked Dave in his mobile home. There were pitchforks involved but the lethal blow came from a defensive knife that went straight through the assailing brother's heart. Needless to say, the job was called off and the last I saw of Dave was on the news, jacket pulled over his head, cigarette hanging out of his mouth, making his way up the steps of the Four Courts in Dublin. He was later acquitted on grounds of self-defence.

It's strange to think back on my time spent amongst these men. I thought of them as different to myself or the rest of the country, waifs and strays lost in a limbo of sorts, their kind only found up around the Border. But that's not necessarily true. I've lived all over Ireland and I've seen these men in every part of it. They are lonely men who live off the fumes of their own braggadocio. Tribal to a man, they believe themselves gatekeepers of national pride; a pride that means you cannot like the English or call it *Northern Ireland*. You cannot be seen to even make a bet on an English football game or say 'we' when referring to the team you support in the Premier League. I wouldn't say they don't care about the Six Counties, or even the thirty-two, but I think the fervour has faded and now it's all about being seen to care. They live in hyper-masculine communities, transitory places – as all border areas are to a certain extent – where they can't let go and can't move forward. The main thing is to appear ready to fight, and with no clear enemy in sight they drink to excess in pubs all over the country and end up fighting each other in petty squabbles that, left too long, grow to such animosity as to not make room for forgiveness.

We're not meant to exist in these in-between spaces. We're meant to pass through – to learn, develop and reconfigure. Staying means living in the tumult of being neither one nor the other. I consider myself lucky in that respect. Though we had a hard time of it when we were kids – the movement back and forth between parents, temporary pledges of allegiance, rows, bust-ups, financial problems, blame cast around in defensive attacks – things managed to avoid becoming so hostile that we couldn't get along. My parents are still amicable, even friendly, and I have two younger brothers and a niece and nephew I wouldn't have had otherwise. Time has moved on and we've passed through to the other side, scratched and scathed for sure, but a little more aware of ourselves. But every now and then I'll get a call from my Dad to tell me about how 'my old friend' has been on the news. I'll be asked if I remember the time we met him in the pub, and I'll say I do, kinda, and we'll agree that he didn't seem much harm back then. The poor cunt just lost his way.

Jess McKinney is a poet from Inishowen, Donegal, and graduate of the MA in Poetry at Queen's University Belfast, where she was awarded the Irish Chair of Poetry Student Award. Her work has appeared in *The Moth*, *The Stinging Fly*, *Banshee*, *SAND Journal*, *Channel* Magazine, *Abridged*, and *The Open Ear*. Her first pamphlet *Weeding* is out with Hazel Press now.

DAMPEN
after Patti Smith

Choked in darkness, the old canal boat aflame
sailed by my window like a swarm of fireflies
lighting up the pines. The sound of it
warmed me out of bed, quiet as a night-blaze.

Slow on saltwater creek, hiss spitting and heavy
with damp. Anointed in kerosene and surrounded
by forest singing evening. Rural noise
without wind and pale lunar moths encircle.

As if my heat-dreams had sprung to life, wheezing
idleness is a form of dying. New thoughts to burn
the old, illuminating the pears just forming,
flushed like a palm in the act of grasping.

I gather what needs to be gathered, knuckles cracking
against the night. Thoughts never far from the children
born as fires burn, into a world where everything
is hopeful enough to make your throat ache.

DISTRACTED KISSES

It is as if, the whole world over, people are tackling the overdue. Conversations, arguments, kisses. Anticipated, dreaded, unexpected. Every night I have been falling asleep to their steady human racket, and when I fall asleep, I become a child again – left uninterrupted in the back of the car until somebody gentle might carry me inside. That is the ultimate act of kindness. Of leaving things be, and sometimes forgetting. Like the sun lounger in the attic, which your aunt bought from a sale at the garden centre. It murders the summer as soon as it's unravelled. These days, there are full days I go without talking – without thinking too deeply – because that is where the fear lives. In rotating the terra firma. I turn the words over on my tongue to gauge the texture, rousing mist instead of sound. My life is more than the story I make of it. I keep writing that down at the start of notebooks hoping something will change. I've read the best parts of life are burnt into the bottom of the pan. It is a good idea, I suppose, to keep in touch with all the people we have ever been. When I listen to god music I know that words can become anything. Bird, sea, birch forest. Can do anything. You think that would be comforting, but no song lasts forever and it's impossible to get those same feelings back. You say it indifferently, I rode the wave just as it was cresting. How does everyone seem to know so much more than I do? Aren't we all just salt in the foam? I throw myself into the fearful ring of your arms without hope of knowing what I'm expecting. Any city can become a home if you climb inside it. I've had some of my best epiphanies in a room with a sink. Where the heavy weather settles like a head- ache. Trust me, it would be too much if you kissed me. It doesn't seem half as bad now that it's morning. Turns out it was just glinting while I was squinting.

DIVING FOR PEARLS
after Nan Goldin

There is a surprise hidden in your opening palm, finger-tips gleaming in the gloom. Sleepy eyed and limbed, you lie in wait while I trawl for godliness, miracles blazing from the very crown of your head. I run my hands back and forth in the sediment, searching for a sigh from some-where – something between ecstasy and grief. This double exposure with a light-bleed. You bide, encased in a bed of mirrors, neon lace and white plaster angels. Never quite able to get comfortable. I let all the grief in the world do the heavy lifting. The biggest stone on the shore carries me to the bottom. These are the shapes our mistakes make in the dark. Desire, anguish, recognition: all but washed from your face, blunted by the shadow of a willow. Over the years, your exact expression will soften in the rain. All the while I am trying to track the pattern of your glances, the easy movement of your arms, that carry those hands for which I'd likely die. Oversized and gentle. Those hands which look like swallows in wind, rain on the horizon, bracken in the shallows. There is electricity in their grasp-ing, where the film singes to reveal a bullet-hole moon shining impossible truth like a flashlight behind every-thing. Creatures, wild things, all gleaming just out of focus. I remember you swearing that photography was the great-est liar of all, second only to poetry. I was just happy to know that we were bound together in sin. But I've thought about it since and it's true – considering all the frisson of those real things – that truth is consistently stranger than fiction. Reality might be our last resort and wouldn't that make it the most romantic of all. Paranormal hopefulness is known to hide in unlikely corners. That just leaves the voice in your head, the one that speaks only truth. It says that I have a story creased into my back, locked between the blades, and it shivers as I descend in one long breath. You and I both know it can only be opened with those hands, and a hunger in your eyes that might consume me; the only thing left in focus. But what would that look like? The subconscious made visible, a historical distance, something deeper than influence. But first, a warning: there is only so much to find that won't end up being about the sea, the sea and you.

HERE IS THE CHURCH

Here is the steeple. Open the doors and there's the people,
standing in the middle of a memory. A couple I met at a
gas station; Hank and Hannah, who were beaming sum-
mer days and never having quarrelled when they asked
me to witness their wedding. The priest wore an Aran
jumper, as per their request, and blessed the small oratory
with sage. It was a sort of holy place, sacred like a morning
no one else has spoiled. Made from planks of salted wood,
and painted sky-blue, it knelt into the Ballyliffin coast.
I arrived an hour early because there was no time set,
and watched a cluster of old women practise genuflecting
next to the pop-up for gluten-free Eucharist. During the
ceremony nobody spoke because no one felt compelled
to. I did not pray because I do not pray, but pledged and
pledged myself to love. We threw sesame sticks – at a loss
for rice – and pretended nothing else existed until the
streetlights came on. The wind was still howling through
the carpark on our way to the hotel for afters. There was
a round of rock shandies for myself, the priest, the old
women winding rosary beads through snapping fingers,
and the happy couple, who were hopping about wildly in
time to a scratched Westlife CD, having given up on the
waltz. Soon the women rose to make shapes like crows in
their long dresses and best hats, swaying enthusiastically
under the disco ball. I watched with my head in my arms,
half listening to the priest renounce his faith, overhearing

the weather come to terms outside. I was halfway through wishing that we would never have to leave when we did. On the car ride home we took a detour through the dunes and I leant against the cool rattling glass, swaying through the cackles of Marge, Mary and Mary-Anne, watching the sky like a child at Christmas. A firework went off in the distance and I wondered why some of them sound more like rain; glad too that some days are great for the parish. Glad that some nights are made uncomplicated, some lives meant for joy, and some embraces for saying exactly what you mean.

JETSAM

We were taking on water when I woke, sinking into the still lake, made strange for all its sea water without a source. The anchor was already over so I kept searching for something else to lose, some divine logic to pull it all together. Next went the compass, then the sails, crates and barrels, foghorn and paddles, the rudder, tackle and bait, lobster pots, driftwood, wattle and swab, sheepshank, cleat hitch and Carrick bend, the cutting wind, choking roots, and bags of sand, your cormorant grace, sea legs, diving rods, lost language, wet symbols, stars fished out of the sky, the hard shoulder, perfect shade of the storm, proof of address, Confirmation names, dried up words funnelled into bottles, what was hidden, sewn into coats, decades of the rosary, knots of dabberlock, the line in the road, the times we touched, armfuls of yellow gorse reflecting your face lowered into the dark, the residue, the constant moon, fluent wings of the deserting creatures I envied, memories certain and not so, each drop in the water a small cherished christening, the stones from my pockets, even the hags with their perfect holes, each one a turning point, even the one with your name on it, finally my own hands, what I was left with and what I was trying to get at.

THE ASSIGNMENT

The assignment was to write about joy (for once). And from where I'm watching the Vaseline blurry screen, you appeared to pluck it from thin air, a starry box of love resting gently in your tender palm. And I know. I know how it sounds and I know, we're playing pretend. But when you tell me to close my eyes, I feel like I have no choice. When you employ me, I make believe. You say, *it is not as simple as imagining what is inside*. The difficulty comes from describing something without holding it. First give it a colour, green maybe, a gentle mist of closeness. Then picture it as a body of water. A quiet lake, rain heavy in the pines, encircling our clumsy campfire where the sun is about to go down and I am reflected in your eyes. Then call it a creature, crashing, small and fearless. A goldfinch. Quaking, sprightly, and full of impossible energy. I tail it quiet as I can manage, and keep reaching until the next thought dispels it – quick as it was conjured. When you ask me whether it can be found underground I am forced to picture the roots I know growing upside down. Breaking cool earth, about to flower into something of the present tense. After all this talk of joy, I am not looking forward to telling you that I forgot about the assignment. That I have not been making a list each night of all the things that make me feel grateful. I got as far as the small, sharp birds, then stopped.

Marcel Krueger is a German non-fiction writer living in Dundalk. Through the prism of family history and his own emigrant existence he explores European history and themes of memory, identity and migration. His essays were published in *The Guardian*, *The Irish Times*, *The Calvert Journal*, and *CNN Travel*, amongst others. Marcel also works as the books editor of Berlin-based *Elsewhere: A Journal of Place.*

A TOPOGRAPHY OF WOUNDS

It is more arduous to honour the memory of anonymous beings than that of the renowned. The construction of history is consecrated to the memory of the nameless.

— Walter Benjamin, 'Theses on the Philosophy of History'

I am not from here.

It is quiet as I walk up Faughart hill. The grey sky of February is hanging low, and it is raining. My walking stick click-clacks on the asphalt as I pass the houses that line the road up the hill on the northern side. They seem deserted, water dripping from the fenders of the cars parked in front. The only other sound is the cawing of crows in the trees on the southern side of the road, and the whooshing of the small wind turbine of the farm building just before the graveyard. I pass the gates of the car park, and before I enter the old sacred grounds, I stop. Straight ahead, north of me, are the rolling fields that frame the entrance to the Gap of the North — or the Moyry Pass as it is also called — in the distance merging with the wooded slopes of the Black

Mountain and Clermont Carn, the highest point of the eastern ridge of the Cooley Mountains. The transmitter mast on its summit, first installed in 1981 to pulse the signals of RTÉ northwards, is obscured by clouds. To my right, south of the ridge, Dundalk Bay opens out into the Irish Sea, bands of rain veiling brighter patches of sky on the horizon. To my left are the brown rocks of Feede and Slievenabolea mountains, marking the beginning of the Ring of Gullion. I can understand why the landscape makes the people born here proud. It is not as breathtakingly beautiful as some of the scenery in, say, West Cork or Donegal, but South Armagh and North Louth have always been humble places, enough in themselves and for the people here. For me, the Borderlands scare.

As a German writer living in Ireland, I sometimes fancy myself a poundshop W. G. Sebald, a grumpy landscape punk with Gore-Tex jacket and notebook stomping across the fields and backroads uncovering the tragedies that have reverberated here for so long. Nothing could be further from the truth. I'm always reluctant to cross fields in fear of farmers with shotguns, I bring my stick to sound on the asphalt to warn the backroad house dogs of my approach, and behind every turn of the road I expect to come across diesel smugglers in balaclavas discarding the poisonous by-products of their illicit trade in a ditch. I do like walking here, but for me the Borderlands always carry an ominous undercurrent. Maybe the reason for that feeling is that this is my first proper border.

The Irish Border. That term contains everything: the War of Independence, the Boundary Commission, smuggling, customs huts, watchtowers, cratered roads, murder, bombs, peace, Brexit. Where I grew up, we needed to give our own lethal border a special name. The 'German border' was something harmless, an easy-to-cross line where jolly, moustachioed Dutch or Austrian border-guards joked with us children in the backseat and wished us 'Happy Holidays'. The *Innerdeutsche Grenze*, the Inner-German Border, or *Deutsch-deutsche Grenze*, the German-German Border, that was the dangerous one. As if just 'German' was not enough to signify the special character of this divide. I was born in 1977 and spent the first twenty-five years of my life in the capitalist West Germany without ever visiting this violent, German-German border. The country I was born in had been divided in 1949, twenty-eight years after the island of Ireland, only to be reopened in 1990. The lethal German-German line with its barbed wire, watchtowers and spring-guns ran across areas that never had any experience of division, smuggling, or murder before: through the German heartlands of Lower Saxony, Thuringia and Hesse, places that had long considered themselves the centre of the German Reich, far from the 'wild' eastern borderlands of East Prussia or the debatable lands of Alsace and Lorraine. I watched this reality of division from afar, through school books, television and the stories of my grandparents who had fled the eastern provinces after World War II. Their stories always ended with warnings that the Russians could come any day, and no wonder: they had seen them come before. There were faceless monsters behind the barbed wire and watchtowers, ready to smash us with their tanks and bombers. The German-German border was a hard but simple one, of which simple stories were told. I could easily distinguish between good and evil from a distance. There was this almost impenetrable Iron Curtain manned with evil, grim-faced communist guards ready to gun down whoever wanted to cross it. The heroes were the simple citizens of the GDR, fleeing to freedom by digging tunnels under the border or flying over it in hot air balloons. Sometimes they died in their efforts.

I did not go to the former GDR until 2001, after 'history had ended' according to historian Francis Fukuyama; after capitalism had won and the danger was gone. I learned about the inner workings of the border in museums and memorial sites, and by then the simple stories had been packaged into an even simpler truth: the GDR had been an inhumane dictatorship in which a caste of old men in cheap grey suits ruled over poor people who had only one wish – to be reunited with free market freedom. And for many years I did not question this truth; Germans cherish clear lines. I had to come to a very different place to start challenging the stories of the country I was born in.

The Irish Border: its eastern lands have a very different atmosphere to anywhere else on the island. It is the first place I have considered 'home' proper; not because I blend in well, I am still the 'German living in town', but because it feels like here I have direct access to the violent fault lines of Irish history. I am very thankful

for my life on this wet and cold island; without Ireland
I would not be writing at all. The stories of its people
and the richness of language here gave me a freedom of
expression that Germany never allowed. I had to leave
my mother tongue to have the courage to pick up a pen.
Always, I try to make sense of the world and my place
in it through history and territory, and this is where
the stories I tell now are always grounded. So it is no
wonder that I am fascinated by the Borderlands. I've
walked them again and again, hoping to decipher some
of the shibboleths and tribalisms of Ireland through the
landscape.

The Hill of Faughart has four stars on Tripadvisor,
and a reviewer calls it 'interesting and creepy', which is
not too far off the mark. After all, it is named after the act
of killing a man. As the 'Táin Bó Cúailnge', our very own
slaughter epic records, it was the place where Cú Chulainn
fell out with his foster-brother Ferbaeth and stepped on
a sharp piece of holly while walking away, which pierced
his leg. He pulled it out, and threw it at Ferbaeth. As poet
Thomas Kinsella recounts in his 1969 translation:

It pierced the hollow at the back of his head
and came out of his mouth in front, and he fell
backwards in the glen.
'That was a throw!' Ferbaeth said.
Some say this is how Focherd in Murtheimne –
the Place of the Throw – got its name.

Faughart doesn't look like much. Viewed from Dundalk, this 113-metre-high hill appears as a green lump in the rolling foothills north of town, just two kilometres south of the Border. Yet before the M1 was blasted through nearby Ravensdale, the main route to the North was always through the Gap of the North; much of the land either side was bog or deep wood. Faughart Hill commanded and still commands the entry to the Gap, and it provides me instant access to this landscape. Not because it is an extravagantly beautiful site, but because of its mundanity, as a place that is today often passed by. It is hard for me to imagine a better place for a cross-section of the martial history and violent folklore of Ireland.

I leave the car park and enter the cemetery. Lichen-covered gravestones stand askew in front of an overgrown church ruin with only the side walls left standing – all under a grey sky – and as always I'm slightly amused by the unintended postcard quality of the site. This is still an active cemetery for the local community, and there are two graves with newer headstones decorated with fresh flowers. As I round the boneyard along the boundary hedges, I come to the ribbons, old blouses, pieces of cloth and corona face masks gently swaying in the rag tree, a laurel growing next to a walled holy well. The well itself is adorned with crosses, pictures of the saints and rosary beads in many colours. The borders between religion and magic are often thin in Ireland, and Faughart is a thin place: the entire cemetery and car park were part of a hill fort in Iron Age times, and in 453 AD Faughart is alleged to have become the birthplace of Catholic saint St Brigid; who is at the same time also Brigid, member of the Tuatha Dé Danann, daughter of the Dagda, and the Irish goddess of poetry and spring.

Right where I stand, under the laurel tree, somebody put a coffin here in May 1999. It contained the mortal remains of Edward Gerard Molloy, known as Eamon, who was not allowed to grow older than twenty-two. He had been pulled from his Belfast home in May 1975, brought across the Border, kept in a mobile home for a short period of time so a local priest could hear his confession, and then – because he was suspected of being an informer – placed in a hollow grave, with a jacket draped over his head, tied with a neck-tie, and shot in the back of the head; the bullet smashing three of his vertebrae and his lower jaw. Twenty-four years after his death, Eamon was given up by the people who killed him, and placed next to St Brigid's Well in a new coffin. He was the first of the so-called *disappeared* to be returned.

Men came to Faughart to die. In 732 AD, the king of Ulaidh, Aedh Roin, was defeated here by the Uí Néill clan and his head was cut off on Cloch an Commaigh, the Stone of Decapitation, which it is alleged is still located near the door of the old church. I do find a slab of granite there that is obviously not a headstone, almost sunken beneath the wet grass. A few steps right of it lies another dead king. Edward the Bruce, brother of Scottish King

MOIRY CASTLE AND THE GAP OF THE NORTH, NEAR DUNDALK.

Robert the Bruce, came to Ireland in 1315, swept away the local English and allied-Irish troops before him, and was crowned High King of Ireland in Dundalk a year later. His reign in Ireland was marked by rampage, pillaging and subsequent famine, so that when he and his army were defeated in another Battle of Faughart in October 1318 not many shed a tear over him. Or, as The *Annals of Ulster* record of his slaying: 'And there was not done from the beginning of the world a deed that was better for the Men of Ireland than that deed.' Though he has a head-stone here and a grave, Edward was allegedly quartered, his body parts sent around Ireland as a warning, and his head delivered to King Edward II in London. I wonder if his bones here are any more real than those of Eamon.

The Borderlands of Armagh and Louth are old ones, complex and often contradictory in nature, and identities and allegiance seem constantly turned on their head. Long before 1921 it was a place of violence, of outlawry, of rebellion. For centuries long before Northern Ireland came into being, Dundalk was the last outpost of English might in Ireland; the men on its ramparts clutching their spears and nervously eyeing the Hill of Faughart in hopes that the wild Ulster Irish would not come. Before the Cooley Peninsula hid anti-treaty IRA men, it provided shelter for United Irishmen fleeing the Ballymascanlon Yeomanry. To me it often feels as if these undulating hills allow history to fold in on itself, making it more dense.

I leave the graveyard and for a moment consider continuing my walk, in a loop that would encompass all the intricacy of this Irish Border. Just down the road are the remains of a Norman motte from the twelfth century. A mile further along the same road stands the grey tower of Moyry Castle; erected in 1601 on orders of English commander Mountjoy after Uí Néill troops left Moyry Pass undefended during the Nine Years' War. Just down the hill from the castle, in a field set back from the road, is the Kilnasaggart Stone, one of the oldest inscribed stones of Ireland. It was set up in the 8th century, decorated with thirteen crosses and bears the inscription, 'This place, bequeathed by Temoc, son of Ceran Bic, under the patronage of Peter, the Apostle.' If I looped back to Jonesborough and crossed the Border to the Republic from here, I would after a while pass the spot where RUC Chief Superintendent Harry Breen and Superintendent

Bob Buchanan where gunned to death with automatic rifles in March 1989, after coming back from a meeting with Gardaí in Dundalk. On the Border itself sits a shed that has one half in the Republic of Ireland, one half in Northern Ireland, and which was used at various times over the last century to smuggle pigs.

I am not from here, and that comes with privilege. As a white male I can walk here more freely than a woman or someone with a different skin colour might. There is also an element of escapism in approaching the tragedies of the Borderlands: I came here at the end of my thirties, neither as refugee nor asylum-seeker, but as someone who decided not to live in my country anymore. I left my Protestant upbringing and all my other childhood traumas safely back in Germany. In Ireland, I never had to face the Catholic Church, never faced unemployment, hopelessness or small town paranoia. I use the landscape to provide me with a framework to engage with the country I left. I still hover between feelings of familiarity and dislocation here, yet it feels as if only at a distance from Germany am I able to form ideas of my native country. And if the Borderlands have taught me one thing, it is that there are no simple stories, there and elsewhere – appearances deceive. Do not look for black-and-white versions of the world: they're not to be found.

Frank Bretfeld was born in 1960 in Marienberg, Saxony. A music lover in his teens, he collected records and kept a file in which he meticulously recorded the names and albums of the rock bands he listened to on western radio. Like many other young men in the GDR, he was drafted into the border guards when he was 18. One night in August 1979, his unit was put on alert as there were fugitives trying to cross his border sector in Thuringia. Frank himself did not see any attempts to escape, but his comrades had to retrieve a heavily wounded fugitive from a minefield who had lost both of his legs. He was so traumatised by this that he committed suicide with his machine pistol while on patrol the next day. Frank, like many others, was not a faceless grey man manning the border, but a human being.

The reality of growing up happy in a communist state, shared by generations of people born in the GDR, has in large part been neglected by the official historiography of German reunification, and their stories laughed at by people from the West, like me. Reunification led to massive unemployment and structural collapse in their hometowns, and the *blühenden Landschaften* – the blossoming landscapes that the new conservative government of a united land promised eastern Germany – never appeared. To this day people in the former GDR feel alienated by a country that told them their previous way of living was now over, and that they had lived a lie. Thirty-two years after David Hasselhoff sang at the crumbling Berlin Wall, German society is still the subject of some antipathy, divided by the former border still. How can I not think of Unionism when I think of this? My hope is that when thirty-two years have

passed after the Good Friday Agreement, the mundanity and magic of the Borderlands will still do their work, even if the Border is gone. Clare Dwyer Hogg expressed this beautifully in the poem 'Brexit: a cry from the Irish Border', performed by Stephen Rea:

> This is what magic in the day to day looks like:
> the spirit of peace in the normality. A gentleness
> in the mundanity.

Victories are often only small, but too frequently they are the only ones we get. As I walk down the hill again I see Dundalk and the old plain of Murtheimne stretched out in front of me, and I'm acutely aware of another advantage of the hill I'm walking down. I recently played around with one of those virtual maps that show you how badly climate change will affect coastal flooding, and if we continue as we do now, most of Dundalk will be submerged in 2050. Faughart will still stand.

Image credits: First image of the GDR border courtesy of Axel Hindemith, Creative Commons CC-by-sa-3.0 de. Second image of Moyry Castle and the Gap of the North courtesy of the author. The third image of Frank Bretfeld with friends before he was called up to join the border troops is courtesy of Private Axel Bretfeld.

John Kelly was born in Enniskillen, County Fermanagh. A first collection of poetry, *Notions,* was published by Dedalus Press in 2018. He lives in Dublin.

THE RAY-GUN

It was plastic with a perfect moulded grip;
silver with a see-through cylinder
and a cosmos of coloured cogs that turned
when you squeezed the trigger.

The best part was the sparks that flew
in the black hole of the coal-shed –
a stone-age mystery involving flint
that also lit the barrel up in sci-fi red.

The trigger, come to think of it,
was crooked, unreliable and made of tin –
when it nipped your finger, the blood
would float, in blobs, from your spaceman skin.

Older weapons couldn't go outside at all –
Colt Revolvers were holstered and forbidden –
but something silvery and space-age
would surely never be mistaken

by an unmarked car or itchy foot patrol.
Not that my constant pal was much concerned –
an army-man with tommy-gun and camouflage
he was always on parade. Saluting. Presenting arms.

One time on the Cam River, we saw a mink.
Boot-black, it bounced through the grass

as my pal took deadly aim. *The law's the law*, he said
and, eagerly, he swore he'd tell the police.

But I said a prayer to a black Peruvian saint
that the bright-eyed mink would get away.
Then the trigger and the sparks
and the sudden shadow of a Martian craft.

THE LONG GAME

We met them in the bush –
painted dogs in all directions –
and, sightings-wise, a real result.
They'd chased a leopard up a tree
and robbed its disembowelled kill,

but all I could see was Ballinaquill's U12s
loosed from their green, enamelled bus,
spilling onto our imperfect grass
in their violent, bony arrogance.
A crooked Border parish famous for it still.

Their arrival was obscene – a yelping chaos
of swerving shoulders and lunging limbs;
the ugly, trotting menace of the one in front –
his too-long neck, his too-large head swaying blindly,
dead eyes rolling for our blood.

Today, our leopard waited in his tree.
Outnumbered, he'd forgo though not forget,
the painted dogs' immeasurable offence.
He'd get them all again – that ringleader for sure –
when, that is, he'd spot the perfect chance.

Maybe next year at the big boys' school,
or on some future blacked-out street.

Or one day, in a poem at dawn,
whispered in the long grass, over coffee,
near the Border with Mozambique.

LAPWINGS IN CAVAN
for Lisa O'Neill

I miss that swerve of road
where lapwings used to muster in the field.
I'd see them and be settled and relieved

and think out loud (Old English)
hleapewince, phillipene,
plover, peewit, pilibín.

Leaper-winker maybe so,
but if ever wings deserved a word like *lap* –
in fact, the only word for it is *flap*

when, haphazardly, they slap the skies
like flying cloths, and even more so
now they're getting scarce.

I wonder what the landmark is
for them – the birds' eye view –
when what they see is annually new.

Is it the bypass or the roundabout?
The applegreen – the forecourt and the lights?
Or just the other pilibíns tumbling in fits and starts?

Somewhere in Pascal's *Pensées*
it says, *How many kingdoms know nothing of us!*
This dwindling kingdom of birds perhaps —

Vanellus vanellus, winnowing fans;
nesting, feeding; flickering above and to the side
of our new and smooth and unobstructed road.

FAMILY

Emily Cooper is a writer and poet whose work has been published in *The Stinging Fly*, *Banshee* and *Poetry Ireland Review*, among others. She was a 2019 recipient of the Next Generation Award from the Arts Council of Ireland. Her poetry debut *Glass*, was published in 2021 by Makina Books.

TREES, HORSES, AND DRY STONE WALLS!

Border Baby
(14-15 January 1988)

It wasn't snowing, but it could have been. There was black ice
on the back road, where the factories now stand, replacing

cow fields and hawthorn trees, and where I first asked
    your Mammy
to marry me. The Drift Inn was closed; fire burnt,
    stools upturned.

We drove fast out of Buncrana, the bonnet bellowing
like a tin-can toucan, agape. Soon the Swilly caught up

with the car. There were swans on the water. Heads submerged
in wings. Some imaginary icebergs drifting aimlessly.

The windows steamed up with your Mammy's breath, I
    wound them down
and pressed my foot to the floor. Bearing down on blind corners.

As we reached the Border, a soldier leaned in through the gap.
I shouted at him 'My wife! My baby!' I cursed and swore.

In Dublin, Seán MacBride was dying and in Israel,
a new war. In Derry I held you for the first time, First Born.

The night before I was born, my parents were out with friends in the Central Bar in Letterkenny. My mother, the designated driver, inconveniently went into labour and was unable to drive my father and herself back to the family home in Buncrana, where she was to collect her hospital bag before going to Altnagelvin Area Hospital in Derry. My father told me the story of my birth regularly as a child, calling it 'The Day You Came into this World'. It was a story that included heroism and swans floating on the Swilly, but conveniently left out the details of the sandwiches he was force-fed to sober him up before getting behind the wheel. It also omitted my mother haemorrhaging, the emergency C-section, and the moment he stopped on the T-junction at Burnfoot to teasingly make her choose which direction to go: home to Buncrana, or to Derry and the hospital; South or North; backwards or forwards.

Despite this dramatic introduction, the Border rarely intruded into my life while I was growing up beside it. My family would cross it often, travelling to the petrol station in Muff for fuel, or to pick up Free State chocolate late at night. Having moved into our farmhouse in 1998, we were there just in time to see the sentry towers removed from the top of the road. We had spent the previous year living in a rented house in the Waterside, tucked in behind an army barracks that was constantly thundering with the sound of helicopters landing and taking off. There was an army checkpoint at the entrance of our street which we had to pass through in order get down to our house. Armoured jeeps would frequently emerge from the barracks, open-topped, with soldiers pointing guns at pedestrians. It was an extreme introduction to Derry.

After being born at home, my parents had taken me to live in London, where they had been for years. They repeated this journey for their next child, my brother, but capitulated on the last two, who were born in England. As an adult, it seems incredible that my mother made that journey at all, flying home alone on both occasions to have her eldest children born Irish. As a child in London, Ireland had meant summer holidays spent swimming at Dunree and Linsfort, short drives from my grandparents' house in Donegal; a very different reality to the one we found ourselves in living at Browning Drive on the Waterside, Derry City. We arrived just as the Good Friday Agreement was being put together, and my brother and I were enrolled in an integrated primary school across the road from us.

The integrated school was an intense learning environment, not necessarily academically, but rather on the subject of identity. We had been brought up in London safe in the knowledge that we were Irish children. We hadn't anticipated what life would be like in Derry in 1997 with a London accent and Catholic parents. There was a rule about not asking other children what religion they were, but somehow this was still the main topic of discussion. We weren't equipped for these questions. When asked what football team I supported, Celtic or Rangers, I picked the one that sounded most like the word Catholic, and was very pleased with myself when I realised I had chosen correctly. My brother was asked whether he was a Catholic or a Christian and he answered confusedly (but correctly) that he was both. I began to change my homework to add in sentence structures that sounded more like those I heard around me, thinking that I could ingratiate myself by adapting my writing. This didn't work, only earning me lower marks and the irritation of my mother.

In London I had been going to the Brownies for years. The whole swearing allegiance to the Crown thing hadn't struck me as strange, but when I joined a local Brownie group in Derry, I soon learned that it wasn't really a Catholic-friendly environment, something I'm surprised my parents hadn't realised. In one session we were asked to draw up a detailed description of ourselves; as well as hobbies, siblings and the usual stuff, they also wanted us to identify our religion – profiling turned out to be a constant thing in Derry – and when I wrote Catholic, my neighbour (a Protestant) whispered to me to rub it out and put in Church of Ireland instead. It transpired that I was the only Catholic in the group and had been unintentionally passing as Protestant with my un-Irish sounding name and accent. Being innately obstinate, I refused and carried on with my colouring in. This became more of an issue when we (the Brownies) went on a cross-community trip with the local Brigín Catholic Girl Guides group. Nothing will make you feel more confused about your identity than going on a cross-community trip with your own community. I stopped going to the Brownies soon after that. I was odd enough without adding to the confusion.

We moved across the Foyle to a suburb called Culmore, just on the Derry side of the Border. We had only come to Derry as a respite between London and going somewhere else. My father had quit his job as a microbiologist and, fed up with London, my parents decided to rent a house in Derry so that we could be close to Mammy's family without changing to a new school system. There was talk of moving to Kuala Lumpur and all sorts of places, but my grandmother was out driving one day and spotted my mammy's dream house for sale.

So without even intending it, we became a family from Derry City living in an old farmhouse with a sagging roof. On moving day, Daddy threw a rope up into a huge old sycamore tree and we were swung terrifyingly high up and down the drive. When it got dark he drove to Muff to pick up chips and cans of 7up, which we ate sitting on the bare wooden floors of the new house. Those huge fat chips soaked in vinegar, and the sparkly citrus 7up is still one of the most memorable meals I've ever had.

We continued to be regarded oddities in Culmore. Not only did we still have English accents (despite my brother practising his Derry accent every night), but we had also moved into what had once been been the post office and, as a result, my brother was now referred to as Postman Pat. His retort – that if he was Postman Pat then why didn't he have a black and white cat? – didn't really stand up once my uncle the vet gifted us three kittens, who quickly multiplied into an army of mostly black and white cats. When other children visited, they weren't accustomed to my mother's eclectic style and would laugh at us for having couches that didn't match. Everyone else had new houses with matching furniture and electrical wires hidden inside walls instead of strung in knotted threads up the stairs.

I was incredulous as to why they couldn't see how beautiful our house was. My father was obsessively restoring the windows, floors and doors himself. He pulled up layers and layers of lino in the kitchen, finding old sandstone tiles, which he removed and cleaned individually to be laid again. The house was giving up its secrets to us, reshaping around our family. Mammy travelled to the auctions and boot-sales in the North, up round Castlerock and Coleraine, finding bargains. The Protestant towns always had the best furniture and she loved listening to Ulster Scots, reminding her of the Parish Speak spoken around Inishowen, where she's from. Overzealous in her bargain hunting, Daddy would periodically hire skips and dump half of it. I was twelve before I got my own bed-room, and only after one of the rooms used for storage was cleared for a visiting family friend to stay in.

Almost as soon as we returned home from London, I became obsessed with horses. Having grown up in a major city for most of my life to that point, horse riding had been an impossibly expensive hobby, but back in Ireland there were ramshackle riding stables everywhere. Testing them out, I went for a hack from one that was housed in the stables of the long-abandoned Boom House under the Foyle Bridge. The horses were kept in stalls with roofs that had caved in; beams half on the ground, half in the rafters. At lunchtime, we milked a goat straight into a cup for the tea. Despite this caution-free environment, they insisted on holding onto the pony I was on for the entire time and I refused to go back, wanting something a bit more exciting.

Motivated by my desire for equestrian adventures – and the removal of one of their four children for full days at a time – my parents would drive me to riding stables over the Border in Inch and Lenamore, picking up other fanatical children along the way. An army of free labour, we spent hours shovelling shit and getting up to no good in the fields along the Border. Teams of us would be sent up the mountains to find ponies if they hadn't been seen in a few days, and we would sneakily ride them bareback down the hills until we were back in sight. These stables were where I had my first kiss, my first drink and, I'm sure, used up all of my spare lives falling off ponies and being kicked in the face. They were also where I smuggled horses across the Border during the foot and mouth crisis.

The drives to the stables during that time taught me exactly where the Border lay, pointing out the landmarks with checkpoints and disinfectant trays. We had to get out of the car so often to dip our shoes that it became muscle memory, pinning those locations in place in my mind. Even now I could draw the Border on a map just by finding Fanny O'Reilly's bridge and Brown's Farm and the back road to Muff past the park that used to be the dump.

Just as we arrived in Culmore, so too did an influx of people from the city. The area had up to that point been predominantly Protestant, with large houses and stone cottages arranged along the edge of the Foyle, down towards the point where a mini lighthouse stands. Large estates were now being built in the barley fields around our house, filling the inside of a large square with cul-de-sacs that had bottleneck entrances around the edges. As children we played in the building sites, smashing windows and jumping in the ditches dug for foundations. But when the estates became more populated, they began to seem like internal worlds. Everyone had their street friends, kind of like cousins; people who were your friends incidentally, because of proximity. The estates felt like foreign territories to us, ones with different rules and ways of speaking. I would take turns visiting classmates in each of them, but I always felt like the fun was continuing without me as I returned to our farmhouse on its own, flanked on one side by a derelict house and on the other by an older couple with grown-up kids. On the corner of our road stood an Orange Hall, which gradually began to be used for things like Irish dancing lessons and local meetings.

The Orange Men would (and still do) march through Culmore early on the morning of the Twelfth, each year dwindling in numbers and increasing in age, though still banging their Lambegs like they were going to war — which I presume some of them felt they were. When we lived on Browning Drive my mother inadvertently joined a parade up the Limavady Road. She was late picking me up from the stables and my father was working in Dublin, but when she got to the top of the road she was met with a sea of bowler hats and bellies. She hadn't realised that the whole main road was shut for hours during the march, blocking residents from leaving their homes. The soldier at the checkpoint tried to explain that she had to wait, but refusing to be trapped, she pushed the nose of our red Volvo estate out and nudged into the crowd, driving in the middle until she could break through and away from the increasingly angry marchers surrounding the car. Her justification for it later was that the English licence plate gave her immunity, just as our Irish one in London had led us to being tailed on more than one occasion.

*

The stables were one of the only neutral places I spent time in. There wasn't much discussion about what religion someone was when we had better things to discuss, be it gossip about who was kissing who or whose horse was actually shite even though they thought it was class. Segregations were mostly around ambition and money. There were those who became successful through sheer force of determination and a lot of debts paid through teaching classes and mucking out stalls, and those who bought their way into it. There were ways of showing off, like how much wood shavings you could buy to mix into your horse's bedding and odd things like using unnecessarily complicated bits. My experience of the stables was a strange mix of hard labour and a bit too much freedom. If we worked hard, we were left to our own devices and we would get up to badness: jumping horses over walls, galloping through any field with an open gate, drinking and smoking weed in the woods.

Every weekend there were shows, jumping tournaments, which meant mixing with other stables and more teenagers to be bold with. These were our cross-community events, where we met horsey people from across the north and into the west. During one show an army helicopter flew over the outdoor arena and landed in the neighbouring field, terrifying the horses, scattering them as they pulled loose from lead ropes and their riders fell off. Beyond causing a fuss during the competition, this was, on reflection, an international incident, seeing as the

British Army had landed in the Republic of Ireland. They must have realised their mistake as they quickly took off again and flew back to Derry, presumably to the barracks beside my old street in the Waterside.

*

Even as the checkpoints and sentries left, the army would still do reconnaissance around Culmore. Walking the dog, you could come across a group of soldiers patrolling the pavements in their heavy camo and guns. Once, a soldier got stuck in our garden. He must have been lost and couldn't contact the rest of his battalion for some reason, because he sat in the corner of the garden hidden behind a laburnum tree all afternoon. My father stood at the front window and stared at him, laughing later that he didn't even have the balls to come and ask to use the phone. I wouldn't have approached my father if I were the soldier. Daddy was a small man but you could say he had presence. Once a local kid tried to break in through our kitchen window. I was woken by our cat, Chubby (my sister had named her when she was a toddler), who always had an air of responsibility about her. She miaowed at me until I got up and saw someone trying to get in. Waking Daddy, I watched as he went down in his underpants and vest roaring. He chased the boy down the road and we had no more problems with people trying to break in. If he'd been a smarter thief he might have realised we never locked the back door.

A few years later, on St Patrick's Day, Daddy was out walking the dog down the point when a boy from the year below me in school started hurling abuse at him. 'Ya Brit! Ya fucking Brit! Go home ya Brit!' The boy, Johnny, had mistaken my dad – a man walking an Irish Water Spaniel with a shillelagh – for an Englishman because of *my* wonky accent. Daddy ignored him and walked home. But the next day as we were driving down the road, he spotted the boy and asked me his name, pulled over and asked, in his thick Belfast accent, 'Excuse me young fella, do you know someone by the name of Johnny Doherty? I heard he was running his mouth about me.' Johnny shook his head, obviously terrified, denying that he knew anyone by that name, and Daddy took off without saying anything more. About fifteen minutes later there was a knock on the door and Johnny was there to apologise profusely, claiming he didn't know that Daddy was Irish and that he was so sorry. He was sent on his way with a warning to be more careful who he was calling a Brit next time.

As I got older, I became more sentimental about Donegal. I never really felt like I belonged in Derry, though I wasn't motivated enough to make the changes that would make me more acceptable. My accent was still inflected by the time I reached my late teens and I had never accommodated the cultural signifiers of the city in the ways my siblings had. My father, sharing my melancholic temperament and overenthusiastic affection for Donegal (he saw Donegal with an admiration reserved for those who didn't grow up in a place), would take me on long drives and walks on rocky beaches, chanting affirmations like 'Trees, horses and dry stone walls! That's what makes Ireland beautiful!' adapting the mantra to suit whatever was more striking that day, be it the sea or sometimes the hills. We'd climb over fences and stand staring at the waves of the Atlantic. It was all very poetic and felt very meaningful, though to apply some sort of metaphor to those experiences might reduce them to something a bit floppy and overwrought. It is easy to present a vision of Ireland that is mystical and romantic, but that's something that makes me uneasy: lazily adding artificial value to something that does not need adornment. Those days in Donegal are simply great memories and valuable on their own. Often there would be grand discussions in the car about everything from art to vaccines to life advice. It felt more like home than Derry, but perhaps that was because I rarely had to interact with anyone whilst walking along deserted beaches with my father, or listening to Mammy dictating her repertoire of family stories as we drove past her grandparents' houses and her father's shop. Those places affected her like Proust's madeleines in architectural and landscape form; she was (and is) unable to resist recounting memories and legends as they come to her.

I didn't want to be from Derry because Derry didn't want me, I wanted to be from Donegal because no one could tell me I wasn't. I had these stories and I could look up at the Mamore Mountains and claim them as my own, my ancestral lands, like some returning American with notions.

It's only now that I am a bit older and sure of myself that I can understand why I clung to that idea of being from Donegal, of belonging to a place that is so beautiful and so empty. I had spent my childhood justifying my identity, always finding that there was something that didn't quite add up to what people wanted from me. Whether it was my accent or my history, I was never quite here, never quite there, so I chose a place rather than a people. Some change their names or affect the way they dress in order to fit their idea of who they want people to think they are. I chose to skip back a generation and ignore Derry and London in order to attach myself to a landscape, one peopled by my ancestors, most of whom were dead and whose acceptance was unrequired.

If people ask me where I'm from I still answer Derry, I don't want to seem deceptive or contrived. However, living on the Border made it impossible to escape a kind of duality; forming an identity that is aware of place and culture in a way that others may not be. It made me consider what it meant to be of a place, not just from it. What are the most important factors: place of birth, heritage, education, or perhaps something less tangible? For my siblings it is simple, they are from Derry, but having had my childhood so cleanly cloven in two, between London and Derry, I have found myself less sure of what I am. If the Border had fallen through the Foyle, there would be no question; the hinterlands of Inishowen would be part of a continuous space that would be easy to define, but the Border existed, and still exists, between our house and Donegal. When I think of home I think of that house in Culmore and of Derry, but I also think of beaches and mountains and those long drives with Daddy, of Football Special in the Drift Inn with my cousins playing cards and of hunting for ponies up the hills.

My father laid claim to Donegal in his own way by being buried there, outside the church in Buncrana where he and Mammy got married. He has a good view of the hills and trees, of some dry stone walls and even horses when they're around. I, on the other hand, moved to a small town in Donegal a couple of years ago and every so often I hear myself being referred to as a 'Donegal poet' and feel a sense of triumph.

Kerri ní Dochartaigh is from the Northwest of Ireland but now lives in the middle, in an old railway cottage with her family. She is the author of *Thin Places*, Canongate (2021), which is currently shortlisted for the Wainwright Prize, and is working on her second book.

FAOI BHUN GLOINE / BENEATH GLASS

snow-feather

mist-light

sand-gatherer

nest-weaver

dawn-bone

moth-time

i

how to word what we have never seen?

how to sculpt it, mould it
carry it, hold it
unearth it, enfold it?

Sure I cannae SEE you

(so I told it)

*

I started dreaming about it less than a month after we first locked down, a little earlier than the North did, on the side of the Border I now live on. It came, at first, in April – the month I have long held the least affection for – a trinity of inner contempt spanning three countries and decades alike.

I say *it*, when to be perfectly honest – despite the fact that the plumage does not easily give anything away in this variety of finch. The differences between the cock and hen as slight as the first vein of light on Solstice. I knew – *ab ovo* – that *it* was a girl.

Not a female bird. It was not a hen finch at all, it was simply a *girl*. A very wee girl, at that. A girl child of no more than three years of age, I would guess. She began to come to me in April 2020 – very early in that fourth month – just as the May began to come to the whitethorn; creamy, newly born. There had been so much whiteness in my world that spring.

I had been, it must be told, re-reading Han Kang's exquisite fragmentary work *The White Book* speaking out loud her list of white things like some incantation or keen. Intermingled, interspecies grief laid bare as spring arrived in the very heart of Ireland.

I took, back then, to making my own list of the season's white things: a seed pink moon, the last frost, a collared dove egg, the skull of a badger, blackthorn, the pelvic girdle of a rat, a pair of hidden cocoons, cabbage whites (in unimaginable abundance) and a season of waning grief.

>But *she* was not white, this finch child.
>She was gold & red & black & tawny.
>She was, this girl, a goldfinch child.

She was, this goldfinch child, a dream.
She came that spring – the one like *no* other
– the one like *every* other – in the dead of night.
And when she came, she sang.

I began to waken from dreams of things I'd never seen with my own eyes but which felt like they could only have been taken directly from my memory – so real and fully lived was their texture.

Dreams of the northern lights above Shroove beach, green & dancing, charged & primal – and it was her – that goldfinch child – who had carried me there somehow.

Dreams of the River Foyle, meandering & inky black, then stopped & frozen – with colossal whales singing up to us both from beneath the ice – and her tapping at the solid body of water as if to free them.

Dreams of moths, delicately fashioned & finely painted, graceful & prepossessing – weaving in and out of milking barns & animal yards – flying through walls & gardens, above streams & piles of rubble. The child sheltering them in her beak in the moments when their strength visibly wavered.

> *and all the while this goldfinch girl, this colourful bird*
> *in a spring of white things, filling the night's visions*
> *with her singing ...*

what was there to do but try and unravel it all?

try to find the way back to the beginning?

try to dig the story up at its very roots?

But where might we start when it comes to imagined things?

Where is the foundation stone for invisible, insubstantial objects?

Where was I supposed to look, to find the meaning – if any – of this goldfinch child?

ii

That particular spring – the one that mirrored its pair of numbers like butterfly wings – continued as well we all know, and we found ourselves increasingly held in our places. Some of us in places to which we had only just arrived. Others in places we knew like the backs of our hands. Places, like our palms, that we have carried along with us – deep inside our bodies – all our lives. Some of us kept in the one place, utterly alone. Others were holed up with our families, with strangers, with folk who we may never have shared more than a handful of words throughout our entire co-habitation – at least up to that point. Some of us took to it all like a skylark to the open blue, whilst others of us batted against the restrictions – the unrecognisable world that daily life had become – bashing our heads against walls. Scraping our knees as we tried to claw our way out, any way we could. We had not, apparently, known we were living before these tectonic shifts hit our plate. We had not, it has been said, ever really realised how lucky we were to roam freely across the land.

Of course, some of us continued to roam – as freely as we felt our existence entitled us to. Some of us bent the rules around themselves – twisted them & turned them & blew them into the breeze like dandelion clocks. The numbers rose & rose, like the sea, like a temperature, like the marks a parent leaves behind in graphite on a white wall. Traces of the only visible form of growth their child made as the years unravelled like a spool of thread.

Loss, so much of it – loss the like of which many of us had never previously heard a murmur of – rippled through the places we both knew and did not. It soon ceased to be about just places (if it ever had been) and we realised that the things at stake were not, in fact, *things* at all. Death, isolation, depression, uncertainty, poverty, fear and ache: this was the language of loss. Humans, jobs, money, food, safety, touch and togetherness: this was its inventory.

*

It has changed us, this experience. It is changing us, still. We have no idea when it will end – *if* it will end – we are unsure what 'normal' might mean in the months and years to come. Way back then, at the very beginning, I could feel it moulding me, somehow. I could feel the pandemic's fingers tracing my skin and leaving their mark. The goldfinch child was really only the beginning – a tipping point in the midst of vast, unthinkable change. I would love to be able to steer clear of cliché when it comes to the recollection of her visits (and what I have taken her to represent.) I found it hard, for quite some time, to speak of her. Try as I might that spring, I could not loosen myself from her hold. Even when she left my nights, I found myself still woven into her feathers; the fabric of our beings intertwined. I'd waken from blank, emptied dreams – to light that really didn't quite belong – either to me, or to that place. Light that had no real right to be there, in that moment of such finely wrought and unsettling collective sorrow. Light that felt like it was suspended, not in the air but in an underlying space. A place – like memory – held beneath glass.

In time, I realised that she was, even in her absence, carrying something to me. Something I had left behind somewhere and had not, before this all happened, even realised I no longer had in my possession. It was unusual, you understand, every single ounce of it. Her presence, her absence: *her*, quite simply. In the world outside – the world of mud & movement, birth & death, loss & hope – life continued, in ways that it both always had, and never had before that year.

My new home – an old stone railway cottage, the last dwelling before you reach the bog – gave itself over into the bright, soft hands of May. On the first two days of that glorious month my lover and I sat in the garden we had spent weeks clearing. Our hands red raw, our arms and legs still bearing the marks of our battle with thorns and brambles – this wilderness we had tamed with our limbs, for a wee while at least.

On the third day, just a few days before my lover's birthday, I awoke to a feeling I recognised but could not place. The sense of something either having shifted – dislodged, even – or having, in fact, been extracted from my insides entirely. How one might feel, say, when one wakens after surgery to find that cells, or a tooth, or an organ have been removed from the unseen parts of one's inner landscape. The light, still, was there but there was – in its bright whiteness – something that struck me like a gap. A crack, a clearing, a perforation: there was a hole in the light that morning of the third of May[1].

I went about my jobs, despite the disquietude the morning still held within its white-toothed, clenched jaw. The sorting of seeds in the shed, the feeding of birds at the herb patch, the drinking of coffee in the burning sun, the making of notes in the shade of the sycamore tree. And then – out of nowhere – it came. The moment one might refer to (if one were so inclined) as the *cusp*. The sound muted – and yet still as clear as a moonlit night – of a creature making contact with glass. I looked up from the book in my hands (Oswald; always Oswald in the month of May) and all of it came crashing down, every last shard of it. I could feel the smallest particles embed themselves in my salty, tingling skin. Not the window, of course – it remained firmly in place. The thing that came down was the memory, the knowledge (in one fell swoop, like an injured tree) of what that dreamlike, disconcerting spring was really all about.

*

[1] On the third of May, 2020, I spent the longest time of my life away from the Irish Border: 3 months and a single day. It is, perhaps, the thing I have felt the most haunted by for my entire life. On the third of May, 2020, the Irish Border celebrated its 99th birthday. How does one celebrate or mourn that which is not even real? That which one has, in fact, never even seen?

For there she was, just beneath my bedroom window, that
goldfinch child.
Her wee body mangled.
Her wee eyes opening & closing against the brightness of
the changed world.

I cradled her in the nook of my jumper.
Held her as the beat of her body ebbed away.
This ethereal, fragile creature: gone.

And still: no way to stop the singing of this finch girl.
And still: no means can be found to trace her lines.
And still: no language in all the land to mourn her ghost.

iii

Border

is more ice than snow /
more lichen than moss /
more bone than egg /
more winter than any of the others, somehow.

leaves traces of itself in the woods /
metaphor over simile /
white space in place of footnote /
fragments-shards-gaps-brokenteeth (etc etc etc ...)

gives nothing away / gives no one a say /
becomes ship-edge in dream or drink or drum light /
whistles when the ghost-train strokes its lines & curves /
over & over & over, repeated.

refracts all the light it chances upon /
is the kind of grey that some call dove /
wants to name its first born *as gaeilge* /
a muddied SWAN CHILD on any given lake.

moans in its sleep when the moon is not quite full /
still believes in things it's been battered into denying /
remembers the first time like it was only yesterday /
salt & silt /crack & fuck / BREAK & howl / bleed it all
back out.

is the moment you wake from the fog-thick-night-place /
is (in fact) a foghorn place itself /
is the tinkling of invisible bells in any harbour /
IS THE PULL BACK DOWN TO THE SINGING

*

Border is a finch is a child is an ache is a loss is a line is a
circle is an egg is a bone is a cabbage white is grief is love
is a year is a hundred years is a ghost is a vein of light

beneath glass

Eoghan Walls is a Derry poet. His most recent collection, *Pigeon Songs*, Seren (2019), was a runner-up for the Pigott Prize. He recently published a large translation of Heidegger's verse, *Thought Poems*, Rowman & Littlefield (2021). He lives in Lancaster with 'a platoon of daughters', where he is a creative writing lecturer at Lancaster University.

THE EMPTY HEAVENS

I was sure the clouds housed cloud-people
with eyes of rain, their bodies solid vapour.
Some of them our ghosts, the others angels
treading on loose wisps of cloud-heather.

On my first flight I reached into the toilet
and cried, feeling wet nothing in the hole.
You laughed for an age and then quietly
explained precipitation out the window:

the broad continents of evaporated moisture,
the stratus, altostratus and cumulonimbus,
droplets refracting sunlight under pressure,
to spatter as rain or sink as fog around us.

So I know this is the only world there is,
and jog each day to live here a little longer.
But the odd time I go running in the mist,
I watch the ruddy faces of passing joggers

in case I see some shadow of your face,
out of the blue, headed to some other place.

DICKS

There was little on which we didn't draw a dick,
compassing grey paint off lockers, etching desks,
but mostly inking each other's files or textbooks,

apostles casting cocks across the Sea of Galilee,
Tybalt's terrible shower unleashed on poor Juliet,
dark colossi swung over relief maps of Gallipoli,

some ridged and veiny, some rushed as signatures,
as if to spray our own marks out through the world,
blue tears of spunk on the black-and-white empires.

Not like the shower-room, where we held towels
in puppet shows over our small clusters of berries,
scuttling into the scalding water like guinea-fowl.

Even Big Gerry, who we all knew swung the strap
of a full grown man, would cave in round himself
if Mr Gallagher scraped his boots on the doorstep.

GRIANÁN NA AILEACH

So stoned we couldn't see the walls of Grianán
for smoke, we disputed where the dragon's teeth
had gone, who was fattest, the Argonauts movie
where hydras' teeth turned into skeletons,

then Mo wound his window down and screamed,
all us laughing, but he was right, in all directions
came the dead: informers, uncles, Brits, bog-eaten
to the bone. We left a trail of smoke and CDs

to lie in heather as their skulls sniffed at our bong,
changed tunes, clacked their toes on the windscreen,
spent a few hours out of the cold. I pissed my jeans
watching bone men chat all night with the radio on.

I woke to see a hare in the front seat, deathly still.
Saw her ears twitch, saw her loping down the hill.

FLUIDS

Hats on, mittens on the daughter, cracking forest ice,
I lift the pane to see crystallised leaves on the mud shelf,
briefly hardened fluids, and when she runs on, I rise
to look over the pines where the valley was hacked
in the last great thaw by glaciers; the hillscape itself
a fluid settling of troughs if you go back far enough,
all dinosaurs and roots crushed into substrates of oil,
and my flesh is already one kind of slackening wax,
brimming at my chin, my waist, and I feel the bowl
of brain fluids swell in my throat, limning my eyes,
and I dare not touch my skin in case it sloughs off
in a jelly of tumours, but then the girl calls back –
she has pine cones! – so I jog after her up the path.

SMOO

Spikey, says the child,

                                        her palm on my face,
                slapping the stubble,

        these sundered molars,
lipomas, bitternesses,

                                        this quota of rage

slapping like rainfall,

                slapping all over
                        the windows, the steeples,

                down the mossy gutter,

                                        out past the Border,
                slapping the brambles

                        underscored by hares,
the hedgehogs and foliage,

                                        the unhinging mandibles,

                all their hungry prayers,
                        slapping the groundwater,
                                where the silt bristles,

the rust in the ribcages,

                        the brittle carburettors,

lobsterpotted carcasses,

these horrible tonnages,
all that I have done,
all I have not done,

smoo, says the child,
palm on her own face,

smoo.

THE HARE ON RACECOURSE ROAD

Never thought you'd be digging a pit for your roadkill
this side of Galliagh, but the bare eye of this bony sac
is the coppery stare of your brother, and it's not until

you're a foot in the hole you see the kick of her leg,
gone for the hedge, and now here's you on your back
scraping after whiteness, face deep in the thorny gap,

like a surgeon scraping under the eye for a tumour,
no, more like a man reaching off the side of his bed
for anaesthesia, the bible, for you, and the hare fled

out the other side, little Shitbeard, Satan's Daughter,
Suedehorns, Bitchass, Horse-Faced Rat, Mudfucker,
kicking grit back at you, jacket and face all scratched

and her out by Slievebawn up on the brow of the hill
poised on her hinds, looking down at you in the ditch,
soaking on all fours in the stooks. Your nose twitches.

Maria McManus, poet, is from Enniskillen. She is artistic director of Quotidian: Word on the Street, a literary arts production company. Her most recent collection is *Available Light*, Arlen House (2018). Cross artform collaborations include the libretti, *Ellipses* and *Wretches* with Keith Acheson, and texts for dance theatre productions, *Bind, Epilogue: A Dancer Dies Twice, Dust* and *Turf* with choreographer Eileen McClory.

THE SILENT TREATMENT

There is a coping stone on the bridge between Belcoo and the *Blaic*. Cold, solid stone. There are two sets of four bore holes, into which you can place your fingers. There is a vertical line in between: the Border.

As a ritual, I stuck my fingers into those holes every time I walked across the bridge. You can have one hand and a foot in the North, and one hand and a foot in the South. You can straddle the Border, or step over it. You can be in one place, or the other, or both, all at the same time. Jump and you can be in neither.

Light and shade. Foreground and shadow. The unapproved road. Border. There is violence. Dying. Ambivalence, ambiguity, duality, duplicity, doubles, twinning, the binary, couples, coupling/divorcing, splitting, divisions, here/there, crossings, the separate/the joint, disparities and confluences, both/neither. Look away now if you don't have the stomach for it. But come back. We have been alone. Weary with it. Stay. Say nothing.

I

My back is to the wall and I'm in a corner, trapped beside the old, smoking oil boiler. The dog barked in the night to get us up, when the fumes were so dangerous the whole household might have died of poisoning. Now it's daytime. I don't know what I've said. I don't remember, but I'm winning. My father is slaying and punching me, and I'm winning, because when he is punching me, he is not punching someone else and, coward that he is, he is punching and goading a teenage girl. I feel nothing. Nothing but satisfaction that he's a coward, that he's lost it, that he's pathetic, and I am strong because I feel nothing, and he's out of control – twice my size, three times my age, and he has all the power, and none. Go on. Yeah. You're the big fella now. You really are. Be my guest.

I say nothing. I cover my head with my arms and crouch to protect my stomach and let him get on with it, expecting that he'll blow himself out. I have disappeared somewhere inside myself. All the noise and the blows are far away. The sound of my mother's voice is pleading with him to stop. He doesn't. She doesn't. I want to tell her I'm fine; that I'm far away. I might look like I'm present, but I'm not. I'm above it, looking down, watching. There, and not there. I left the scene with the first hit. This is how I save myself.

It is me now, another time it'll be someone else. This is how we save each other. Stepping into the line of fire, one at a time.

II

There is a shot. Several. A man is screaming like a wounded animal at our front door in the night-time. 'Let me in. I've been ambushed. I've been ambushed. Let me in.'

There's a strategy, a code for situations like this. A woman will go to the door and open it because a woman is less likely to be shot. This might be the trap – the 'ambushee' might be the ambusher. We don't know. Are we hostages? We don't know.

Doing nothing is an option. We could hear all of it and pretend we are hearing nothing and just do nothing and leave him there. We could stay still and silent and hear it all. The response could be no response.

But this isn't who we are and when someone terrified, armed, firing a gun and screaming turns up in the night-time, we open the door and let him in. Think what you like. However contradictory, however absurd or conflicting, however counterintuitive, believe behaviour. We open the door and let him in.

My mother opens the door to the screaming, gun-toting stranger in the night-time. Seven of her eight children are sleeping upstairs. The eldest, aged eighteen, has emigrated already and is three and a half thousand miles away. She is 'awayaway'.

It's the first time I've seen my father completely naked. His silhouette in the dark. I shouldn't be seeing his penis. You might say, I shouldn't be looking. But I am, and I do.

The phone is on the windowsill at the top of the stairs. The door to the girls' room is open. My bed is beside this open door. And there he is, dialling 999, naked.

Emergency, which service please?

In the night. My naked father is telling the emergency services that the man with the gun is a cop; that he has been ambushed round the corner from our house, down near *the plantin* – a coppice of trees, round the bad bends and at a dip in the road four miles from the Border. He was going to Belcoo to go on duty at 4 a.m. He has driven from Lurgan, or Lisburn, or somewhere.

They will not come. Emergency services will not come. The police will not come to get their man. The army will not come. And nobody has been injured, so there won't be an ambulance either. This could be a trap. They might all get ambushed. Lured out into the dark.

Who's to say my father is telling the truth? Who's to say that there isn't another man with a gun to my father's head, telling him to tell them they have to come? So they can be shot. Who's to say there aren't more men outside in the dark with guns? Who's to say?

Their man is not injured. There's no need for an ambulance. No one got hit by the shots. *But he is agitated and restless and has a gun in his hands. There are children in this house.* Do nothing until first light. Nothing.

The man won't put the gun down. He paces the floor with agitation. My mother, my father and my oldest brother are in the living room with the terrified man, the loaded gun. The police will not come.

The house is in darkness because the ambushers might be still looking for him and here he is, in a house of children, in the dark, with his gun. All the children in the house are moved from the boy's room above the living room to the girl's room above my parent's room. Don't move. Don't come down. Don't look out. Keep the lights off. *Can we have Santa up here?*

Santa the alert-dog, patron saint of dodgy boilers. Santa, the Geiger counter of our father's nuclear temper. *What humour is our father in today, Santa? Are you still on the sofa, Santa? Or are you behind it? Are you under a table? What is the speed and amplitude of that wagging tail? Eh? Here boy.* Santa of the wonky front flipper-like leg and the wonky back leg, straight where it should be bent. Santa with the black fur and brown dog-eyebrows and white tip 'tail-light'. Santa, who is never allowed up the stairs ... is allowed up the stairs.

At dawn, they come for the man. The police come, not the ambushers. We're allowed downstairs when they go and we're told to get ready for school. Never mind not sleeping. Never mind the fear. Carry on as though nothing happened. Something might have happened but didn't. Nothing happened. Things do, but not here, not now. Get on that bus. My mother tells us she'll kill us if we say one word about what happened this night. *Not one word. Not today. Not tomorrow. Not in ten years' time.*

Never. Doyouhearmeareyoulisteninnevernevernever. Never. Youcouldgetusallshot. We must say nothing and keep on saying nothing. We can sleep together, five, six, seven to a bed for as long as necessary, if and until, we feel able to drift back towards our own beds, or our own sides of the bed. Only some people have a bed to themselves. Santa is back downstairs.

III

Jack Havlin is ranting. *He's rarin' up*. He's doing what he always does, which is ranting; his wristwatch is off. It's on the pulpit in front of him. He puts it down, face propped up, timing his sermon, then lifts it, rolls his hands over one another around an invisible hub, the expandable wristband rolling over one back-hand after the other. It's like a Ferris wheel. Or a hamster wheel. He shouts, bangs his fist off the wall beside the pulpit again and again. The watch is across his palm now. He puts it down. Bangs his fist off the wall again and then massages his right hand with his left to rub the pain away. But it's all noise. *Jack, it's all noise. No one cares.*

On the odd occasion Santa wanders into Mass, I'm glad of the distraction. An excuse to leave: *I'd better go and take this dog home. C'mon Santa. C'mon boy*. Encouraging the dog to come to Mass doesn't work. He's too smart for that. He has to come of his own accord. Nipping in when some latecomer doesn't close the door properly.

Father Jack is Bowie-esque. He has peculiar hair. Fine, blond-red hair and translucent skin. The comparison begins and ends with his hair. He rants, but his Masses are quick. Which is good.

The other priest, Father Slowey's masses are ... slow. Boring and slow.

Jack Havlin, *Father Quickie*, is a Belfast man. An Ardoyne man. An angry man. Another one. He hates

people. He hates us. He hates being here. He hates every-
one and treats us like stupid bovine country people.

'Sure Father Jack be's bad with his nerves,' they say.
'Sure, they stuck Jack Havlin out here where he could do
no harm, because he probably couldn't hack it up yonder
in Belfast. The ones in Belfast wouldn't put up wi' the
like of that, sure they wouldn't. But they think they can
send anyone out here. Who else would put up with him?
No one. Sure, he's pure mad so he is. Pure mad.'

So when Father Jack is ranting about policemen and
a bomb in a field down by the lough, it's not much differ-
ent than him ranting about people coming late to Mass.
'It was a horrible sight. I was sickened. I was sick. I was
sickened and all I could do was pray for them and try to
comfort people at the scene.' He'd been on the telly, and
now here he was again. In front of us. *No one is listening,
Jack*. No one can hear for the shouting and the noise. We're
here for the cabaret. And because we must. Every Sunday.
Not just this one. Now, when we should be listening, we
can't hear for the shouting. We can't hear the silence. Can't
hear the unsaid, the unsayable. Can't sense who among us is
missing a heartbeat, holding their breath, brazening it out.
The accusations. Who among us is smugly satisfied by this?
Who knows something? And why would they tell you?
Nobody cares that you're bad with your nerves. No one.

Nine people died that same day. In three different inci-
dents. Three of the nine died just four miles from here.

IV

Soon after, the RUC offer the youth club day trips to Portrush and Portstewart. There will be minibuses, they say. The British Army will feed us chicken and chips from the back of a 'Paddy Wagon'. My mother will not want us to go. We will beg to go. She will say, 'They'll only be looking for information from youse.'

We'll say, 'We don't know anything. And we can't tell them anything because we know nothing. And we never get to go anywhere. A school trip to see Blessed Oliver Plunkett's head in Drogheda doesn't count. It was horrible, so it was. It was hard to tell it was even a head.' Blessed Oliver Plunkett was beatified in 1920. He was to be canonised a saint in 1975, so we had a 'get-in-ahead-of-the-crowds' sort of school trip. St Peter's Cathedral in Drogheda.

'None of your Euro Disneys back in the day. What do ya want; jam on it?' the people in Belfast ask when they mean one shouldn't ask for more. Well we got jam too. At Mellifont Abbey. And postcards of Oliver Plunkett's head. We crossed the Border near Monaghan. The bus stopped at a Sisters of Mercy primary school so we could use the toilets. A nun herded us together and offered that her class could sing a hymn for our class.

'Do you want to hear them sing a hymn for you? Hail, Glorious St Patrick? Hmmm?'

'Ye-sssssss, sister,' said everyone. Except me. One small 'No Sis-ter' stood out. 'Who is that very rude girl? Who is she? Who said no?'

Me. I slid my hand up. I *thought* 'no'. I *meant* 'no', but hadn't realised that the voice in my head, was the voice outside my head; the voice that said, *No-oh, Sis-ter.* Sometimes even nuns don't want the truth.

I'd been elsewhere – distracted, feeling nauseous with travel sickness; nausea fuelled by the prospect of visiting a three-hundred-year-old skull in a glass case. Oliver Plunkett got his head in his hands for telling the truth.

'So can we Mammy? Can we go with Billy the cop?'

Billy the cop came to offer a trip to the north coast to the youth club. People like Billy because he's friendly. And anyway, if they ask me questions I'll tell the truth, and that'll be nothing, because I know nothing. There's nothing to tell.

We go. There are beaches in the North. Until then, all beaches were in Donegal – Rossnowlagh, Bundoran. What I learn from the cops is that there are beaches in the North and some of them have black sand. What the cops learn is that some kids go on the trip. Others don't.

V

'Who was that fuckin' eejit at Mass tonight?'

I had not been to Mass. I didn't know the answer. Jim, the Garda, the boyfriend of my friend, is asking this question. We're all in the back bar of The Bush, in Blacklion – the *Blaic*. It's winter, the Feast of the Epiphany. *Nollaig na mBan*.

This is our spot. The back bar, the far back corner of the back bar to boot. It is comfortingly, dimly lit. A banquette right round the walls. Images of Martel's speleological maps of the Marble Arch Caves on the walls. The underworld. Here's where the cavers hang out, enthusiasts and experts from elsewhere, various students of the Caving Club at Queen's University. And here's us: 'home for the weekend' students, a few underage drinkers, off-duty gardaí, customs men, prison officers from Loughan House, farmers, locals from the North, locals from the South. A lot of unsuitable men. There are pints of Guinness. Glasses of shandy. Harp. Smithwick's. Black Russians. Bacardi. Pernod and white. Red lemonade. Ginger ale. Hot whiskies. Hot ports. There are bags of Tayto (southern Tayto, naturally) torn open in the centre of the table, for sharing. There's a round metal ashtray, branded with a logo of some beer or other, bunged with fag ends. There are packets of cigarettes. Major. Silk Cut red/blue/menthol/Purple King-size. Take your pick. Carrolls. Embassy Regal. Embassy Reds. Boxes of Bo-Peep matches. Swift matches. Swan Vestas, Ship's, Bryant & May's. Brown heads and red heads. Small pools of spilled beer. Beer mats. Sodden or torn. Dry beer mats for 'flip and catch', for building towers. The thick fog of smoke.

'Some fuckin' eejit, talking back to the priest. In Mass. Shouting back at the priest,' says Jim, the off-duty Garda.

'Our ones were at Mass and nobody said about it. What happened?' I ask my friend. 'You were there. Who was it? How could our ones not see that? Say nothin'?' No one says anything. The conversation ends.

Within a week, the Gardaí get a message from Dublin that they're not to be crossing the Border, off-duty or otherwise. Mass or no Mass. Girlfriends or no girlfriends. Not in civvies. Not at all. Orders from Dublin. End of.

The story had travelled – and as is the law of unintended consequences – rounded back again. No socialising in the North. Go the long way round to Bundoran or Ballyshannon, via Manorhamilton, not Belcoo, Garrison or Belleek. Go to Carrick-on-Shannon or Sligo instead. Or, God forbid, Glenfarne. Mohill. Dowra for nights out.

They were rookies. They didn't want to be in Blacklion anyway. When they'd got their postings after passing out of Templemore, some of these country boys thought they were headed for Dublin. There were at least two pubs in Dublin called The Black Lion, but they were not this place. They were not the *Blaic*. A one-horse town. Literally, one horse. A frontier, with a supermarket, a post office, half a dozen pubs, 'spirit-grocers', a fire station the size of a garden shed, John Bluff's shop, Gilmurray's, Harold Johnston's.

There were other things the Guards didn't like. They didn't like being sent round the village to check for dog permits. Nor manning the checkpoint on the main street, the corner at Peadar Green's Bar, checking cars and drivers' licences. Getting taunted by the locals if they were sent by the Sergeant to raid the pubs. They'd start at Brian Dolan's, or Frank Eddie's, or Green's. They'd always do The Bush Bar last so there was time for word to get round, so they wouldn't have to be throwing us out of the pub. Taunted, the hats knocked off them from behind their backs. Signing passport forms:

'I know, I know you, and I know you say who it is you are, but you could be anybody. And sure, what would we know?'

And they didn't like having to carry guns when they were sent out on searches for Dominic McGlinchey when he went on the run. They were glad that when the shoot-out finally happened, it was near Dundalk and not here.

'I never joined the Gardaí to be carrying guns. That's not what I got in to this for at all.'

VI

My father: 'Her nibs is givin' me the silent treatment. The Minister of Home Affairs has moved to the War Department.' He had swagger. Relished confrontation and anti-authoritarianism, except of course when we stood up to him. He didn't like that at all.

The silent treatment. It took days before the story emerged. My father hated the parish priest so much he regularly drove fifteen miles to go to Mass in a monastery in order to avoid him.

'Get out that door,' he'd say, ordering us out and down the road to the local church. 'Get out that door and get to Mass, for you're none too gospel-greedy.' Then he'd spend a quiet hour sitting on his arse. He commandeered the armchair nearest the fire, clumping it across the woodblock floor, stretching his arm out and reaching to poke the buttons on the TV with 'Jackie', an old blackthorn walking stick. He wouldn't stand up to change the channel. He even had a short cut for that.

The walking stick was something he was given/ stole/got from Jackie McNulty, a local undertaker in Enniskillen. Jackie and his brother, 'The Badger' were the go-to people to get 'dibbled-in'.

He broke his own rules. Not only did he go to the local church on the Epiphany, but he was drunk. And late. He despised Father Jack Havlin. And Jack despised everyone. This night, his rant was about latecomers. 'There is one day and one day only a priest can say three masses and that is on the feast of the Epiphany. This is my third Mass today. I have been on time for every one of them, and you people can't even turn up on time. Standing yonder at the back. There's plenty of seats. Here!'

He pointed at all the empty seats at the front of the chapel, and at the herd of people at the back. He'd only started and was puce with rage.

'How do you know?' said my father. He was, according to my mother, sitting near the back, his arms folded. His face flared and ruddy with drink and belligerence. She and my brother were mortified.

'What?'

'I said, how the fuck do you know we've only been to one Mass? You know nothing about what anybody here has had to do today. How the fuck would you know? People could have been out working.'

'And some people wouldn't know what a day's work was. If the cap fits ...' was Father Jack's retort.

When the subject of the Epiphany came up again, my friend admitted she'd thought I was bluffing when I denied knowing anything.

VII

I had a bay mare when I was a teenager. Her show name was *Say Nothing*.

VIII

There's a coping stone on top of the bridge between Belcoo and the *Blaic*. There are two sets of four bore holes, into which you can place your fingers. There's avertical line in between: the Border.

I stuck my fingers into those holes. A hand and a foot in the North. A hand and a foot in the South. Straddling the Border. Step over it. One place or the other. Both at the same time.

Jump | Neither.

Séamas O'Reilly is an author from Derry who writes mainly about culture, the internet, politics and family. Alongside regular columns in *The Observer* and *Irish Tatler*, he is Features Editor of *The Fence* Magazine and a regular contributor to *The Irish Times*. His work has appeared in *The New York Times*, *The Guardian*, *Vulture*, *VICE* and *The New Statesman*. His first book, a memoir entitled *Did Ye Hear Mammy Died?*, was released in July, 2021. He lives in London with his wife, son, and their numerous streaming TV services.

SLEEPOVER

On the day of the sleepover, my father and I were heaving tarps into the garage when the Dineens' car arrived. Daddy walked over and leaned in but, by then, Mick was already opening the door and Phillie had bolted, terrier-like, from the car. Daddy lifted his hands from the inside frame of the driver's window, straightened his back and resigned himself to conversation.

'They're long gone, Pat,' Mick said, smoothing the car's roof like a bedsheet as he stood. Phillie picked up the football at my feet, thumped me on the shoulder, and set off running into our field. I loitered on beside the men, scuffing my trainer on the gravel hoping Daddy would give me a fiver for the day, which he sometimes did when Mick was around.

'What in under a God?' my dad said with concern, before asking how many had been stolen. It was early summer and both men faced each other with pocketed hands, withdrawing them once a minute to swat, King Kong fashion, at the thought balloon of midges which formed above their heads.

'Nineteen ewes. Thirty lambs. Broke the hurdle on the way out for a good time while they were at it.'

'Tiernan was the same last week.'

'Long gone.'

'This is it,' my dad said, sucking air with his cheeks and tutting. He did this any time he couldn't think of a better sound to make, which was often with Mick Dineen.

Mick's talk ran to sheep, Gaelic football and bombings, and since we were the only family for miles that didn't rear or play, the first two subjects were out. The third was more or less defunct due to an uncharacteristically fallow period in paramilitary activity. This dismayed both men; Mick as an arch republican, and Daddy as a man left flailing at flies in a conversational desert.

'Guards no use?'

'Not at aallll,' Mick said, as if my father had suggested he reach out to Batman. 'Sure they'd be over this side by now anyway.'

Daddy knew more than to ask if he'd pass details to the RUC.

We were the first house in Derry along the Letterkenny road – the Dineens' ten minutes east into Donegal. The separation was in name only, since the UK checkpoint had been moved a few miles west to Nixon's Corner, and the road continued uninterrupted from South to North without mention. The only sign that you'd have traversed an international frontier was a small, pockmarked rectangle welcoming travellers to Derry, or rather – as was ubiquitous for all such signs from there to Glenshane – ███████derry.

Outwardly, our lives were as identical as any two families separated by a mile of open countryside. Me and Phillie went to Derry schools and numbed our bodies playing football – foreign football – in scraggly pitches around Donegal. Our dads got the local messages in the Free State but the big weekly shop was paid for in pounds sterling. We watched the BBC news, but *The Late Late Show* was on Friday nights, and *Eurovision* was RTÉ coverage only – on pain of your remote-control privileges being revoked.

Differences remained. My father was quiet, thin and rough in the Derry way. He was a replanted city boy whose trade changed with the seasons. His year was divided up into ice creams and fireworks, solid fuels and Christmas trees. Only the red diesel persisted throughout, not least his bespoke trade in washing it through a pump and six sieves until the red turned clear.

For a time, he operated the petrol station half a mile to the west, but he sold it off once the price in Killea dried him out. The outfit that owned the plot now sold pallets, fireplaces, licence plates; all those strange, disconnected things country people like to sell in one place for no good reason. My dad would never again cast a shadow on their courtyard, but since they knew better than to sell diesel, trees or ice cream, something like détente was observed. They were Brennans from Carrigans but everyone still called their site Maguire's in reference to us, which irked Daddy but pleased me for reasons I couldn't place.

Mick's work was less varied. He farmed and was the coach of the local football team, for whom his eldest, Declan, played. Phillie, however, did not, even though he always referred to it as his 'boys' club' – as if Phillie would be turning away from soccer any day now. Mick was rough in the Donegal way. His skin had been creased and folded by fifty listless summers, and he had hands so huge and rough they looked sore. He was short but powerfully built, with arms that could throw a medicine ball over a shed. I made Daddy laugh once by saying he looked like a caveman from the cover of a *National Geographic*. I said this many times afterward too, but future retellings never had the same effect. He preferred to say Mick looked like someone who'd been 'rode hard and put away wet'. At this, I laughed every time.

In person, he would mimic the hardier countryman's stance, mirroring his body language and uttering non-committal tics to speed things along. Daddy was uneasy around people who talked to him unprompted. It was the kind of pensive brooding that was apparent when you watched him talk with enough sheep farmers. The kind that made a chatty nine-year old measure his words.

'Anyway,' he said, pulling out his wallet and proffering me a fiver like it was something he did all the time without thinking.

'This is for the day. Good luck, Mick!'

'I'll have him back in one piece. Be seein' ya, Pat.'

Phillie was running behind me, excited by a broken go-kart he'd seen in the garage, where Daddy kept a perilous assortment of car parts, tools and enough random pig iron to build a statue of himself. He barked at me to clear Phillie out.

'If he breaks his leg, it'll be me up in court.'

Mick laughed like this was the funniest thing he'd ever heard my father say, because it probably was. He slapped the car roof, started the engine, beeped his horn and we took off.

In the back of the car, Phillie too declaimed on sheep. When we were in mixed company, at football or the bus to school, he never talked about sheep, but when we were alone it was always his starter, since he'd worked out that it was something about which I knew little, and he liked to have that over me. I'd try and talk about books or cartoons or the smell bleach made when it had rinsed out a four-month-old tray of ice cream, and he'd change the subject to hoggets, hard ground and rustlers.

That and VHS tapes. Phillie had seen *Kickboxer* and *Hard to Kill*, and knew a man who had been Steven Seagal's trainer in America who said he could kick a deck of cards so that the Ace of Spades landed between his toes.

'Yer man, the trainer?'

'No, Seagal. He does it for the craic.'

'Jesus.'

'And to impress chicks. He's mad for the chicks.'

'Wow.'

Phillie knew all about chicks. My sister Niamh, away at Magee studying nursing, was a fine chick, he said.

He knew this because he was worldly. Fast approaching his tenth birthday, he'd grown out of tree huts, sticker albums and Power Rangers, all of which he considered 'very gay'. So, we got on with discussing stolen sheep and Steven Seagal's way with women.

We stopped in Killea and Mick stepped out. He returned with ices, a ham for dinner and a bag of briquettes which were furtively placed under the driver's seat before he handed us our Golly Bars.

'Forgot to ask your dad!' he said, with a smile that suggested he wasn't a man who forgot, or smiled, very often. I knew my dad's prices. I was just delighted to have an ice cream in my hand and a fiver in my pocket; the thrill of an untouched future.

When we arrived at the Dineens' house, his mother gave me a hug, which was usual, and a tour of the bedroom, which was not.

'You'll be there,' she said, gesturing to Phillie's bed like I was a visiting dignitary, or a drifter from a story who goes house to house making soup from stones.

'Phillie will have the camp bed on the floor, won't ye Phillie?'

Phillie said 'aye' before plonking my bag on his bed and giving me a look that clarified he would not, under any circumstances, be sleeping on a camp bed.

I had never slept over with the Dineens. I'd never slept over anywhere, but Martina had thought it was a good idea since we were such good friends. She'd had a front row seat for the entire duration of our acquaintance and discerned within it the sort of bonhomie you rarely see outside of war. In fact, Phillie and I endured a friendship that hadn't so much grown as developed since childhood, like a stammer or diabetes. We were a horse and donkey put to pasture in convenience. Every house around us was half a mile apart, and the cumulative population too old to sustain a viable marketplace in nine-year-old boys. It was a scarcity economy, so ours was a friendship scavenged from scrap.

We had four years to develop a connection that spanned outwards from utility, but none emerged. He was six months older than me which, at our age, proved an often insurmountable gap. Our first few hangouts were tentative, an ember of something trying its best to catch fire. Sometimes it smouldered into a feeling just about approaching fondness, but the smoke never lingered, and we'd land back in an inert acquaintance which was only made stranger by how much time we spent with each other.

Despite this, our friendship seemed important to Martina. It may have been one of the primary fixations of her life. She was constantly saying we were 'thick as thieves', or 'getting on so well', even if we were sitting in sullen silence, sharpening small or big sticks to throw at hay bales, or at each other.

Martina Dineen liked me more than anyone else in the family. She probably liked me more than anyone in my own. As far as she was concerned, I'd hung the lights on the Letterkenny road. When I was visiting, she'd fold clothes two whole rooms away from the dryer, laughing at everything I said.

'I'll get out of you boys' way so you can have some fun,' was a common refrain, as if our riotous connection would flourish to even greater heights outside her presence. Of course, she never actually left, preferring to wipe surfaces or fold Mass cards about two metres further away; all the better to bask in the full wattage of our rapport.

I was reliably informed – by Phillie – that she talked about what a nice boy I was all the time, or correct his grammar and say, 'Conor Maguire would never say "amn't"'.

I suppose he meant this as an insult, but I was delighted. He didn't mention her saying, 'the way you treat me, and wee Conor with no mother' or 'the pair of them rattling around without a mammy in the house, poor critters', but I presumed she did say these kinds of things because she very nearly said them to me herself. Phillie even got close to telling me once or twice. On those occasions, I would see the mental effort it took for him to avoid doing so, and I was always delighted once he dispelled the impulse with a punch to my arm, or a lascivious remark about Niamh.

We spent the rest of that airy summer evening shepherding midges around every acre of the farm, chasing each other and poking things with sticks. We were soon drenched in puppy sweat – me worse than him since I never removed my T-shirt. Phillie was happy to discard his top once the fields went soft. He had a lean, powerful body for a ten-year-old, and was as close to having a tan as anyone from Donegal could reasonably claim. Outside of bathing, I never went topless at all, so my freckling stopped just above my elbow and stood in such contrast to my perfectly cotton-white body that my arms looked like second-hand limbs, transplanted on to a factory-fresh torso.

With his shirt off, I could see Phillie's scar. It ran from just below his armpit to just above his last rib, on his left side. He'd fallen in a cattle grate and always said he didn't like to talk about it. He said this so frequently that I guess I asked about it too much. The scar was bright white; thin and clean and smooth but also lumped with little rivulets of texture, like batter that had set in clumps, or a child's first attempt at decorating a cake with a piping bag.

Phillie showed me where the sheep had been taken, the tyre tracks and the broken gate. He called the rustlers *bastards* and told me they'd butchered Tolands' there in his field. He made the slice mark over his scar, for emphasis, and I wondered if he'd practised this.

'This is a crime scene,' he said. 'And when we catch the bastards who did it there'll be another one.' This I knew he'd practised, because it was the first time he'd ever said anything about sheep in the same voice he used when talking about Steven Seagal.

When we came in, Martina winced at the wet dog smell, but in the face of our contentedness she was forced to declare again how great it was that we were getting on so well. She tutted at Phillie for wrecking his own top,

243

filmed with grease and grass, but smiled at mine even though it was significantly worse. She dug in her basket and soon we were dressed in clean shirts, both of them Phillie's. She handed it to me like it had long been her dream to dress me well.

As we sat down for dinner, Phillie quietly said, 'You don't have to stay over if you don't want to'.

I smiled and said that I wanted to, but I was lying. Some expiry in my heart had passed. Ordinarily, time spent with Phillie had fixed boundaries. Four hours spent playing football, poking cow turds or asking him about his scar would pass in an instant. The process of discovering that we could not, after all, select a specific playing card with our foot by kicking the entire deck, could occupy an entire afternoon. Sitting down to eat with the Dineens who – it turned out – didn't even listen to the radio throughout, felt different.

I asked for butter and discovered, to my horror, that this was a house where they ate their spuds dry, which made Martina's jaunty 'not to worry' trot to the fridge feel like she was fetching me one of her own kidneys. Phillie said little and Mick said nothing at all. At the best of times, Mick regarded every word I spoke with gentle confusion, as if I were a fence he was sure he'd only mended recently, but which somehow needed mending again. Now, I was simply ignored.

Martina was always concerned about my father, and I was grateful for the opportunity to lie in his defence.

'He's selling fuels in Dungloe some of the week, and Bridgend the rest.'

'Is he, right enough? And would there be a lot of work in that?'

'Back to front, Mrs Dineen, back to front.'

'Grand so,' and turning to Mick. 'You should get some off him, Love, before they all go.'

There was a pause before Mick said, 'I will, aye,' and looked back at his ham.

'Seems like they're flying out,' Martina said, but after much too long a gap. I felt a pull toward my own small world, as all the time in the universe was slowly pumped through six sieves. Talk soon turned back to rustlers, insurance forms and broken gates.

After dinner came a listless game of football and a double bill of *Gladiators*, in which Australian Gladiators fought alongside the British ones we knew, and in such a way that it was presumed we would know and care who they were. Phillie and I grew restless on the couch, devoid of enthusiasm for the antics of off-brand muscle-men like Cougar and Vulcan, but also having met some terminus in our tolerance for each other.

Bedtime came as strange relief, a chance to escape the clumsy tension of a family whose balance had been upended by my presence. Toothbrushes were presented and we were ushered into the comfortable discomfort of Phillie's bedroom, which seemed strange in the glow of the dark. It dawned on me, with horror, that I was to wake up, brush teeth and have breakfast in a place that was not my own. I would, I thought, simply go without butter if I had to.

In bed, my head swam with the otherness of everything around me, the moving sheets from Phillie in his bed, tense and awake as I was. I felt for the first time like I was in a foreign country. One of the legs on the camp bed had buckled so my wrists brushed the carpet as I turned in search of sleep. I became overwhelmingly conscious that the silence from his bedroom window was not the silence of my own, supplemented by house-sounds and pipe-creaks that were alien to me.

My hand was on my bag before I even realised I was lifting my body out of bed. Phillie sat up and said 'alright' so I left the room without a word. Out the back door and down the drive, I started running. Toward the comfort of guilt-free butter, and silences I recognised, toward fridge-hums and clock-ticks I knew, down the unlit ditches of the Letterkenny road, through the back of Tolands' and Tiernans', past the broken tractors in Campbells' yard and the truck parked overnight beside the tile factory at the Border.

I shimmied through the hedges and briars of Wards' pasture, cutting Phillie's shirt as I sliced through brambles on the soft mire facing our house, past the horse, past the donkey they gave the horse to keep her company, and over the fence until I was yards from my own darkened house, framed in light from the still-illuminated garage inches from my face.

I pushed open the door. I heard tools drop and the rustle of plastic sheeting. I realised for the first time that I was crying.

'Ah pet, what's the matter?' my father said, as a lamb's leg dropped by his foot. He scuffed it under tarp with one rough boot as I ran into his big, bloodied arms.

Annemarie Ní Churreáin is a poet and writer from Donegal. Her publications include *Bloodroot*, Doire Press (2017), *Town*, The Salvage Press (2018) and *The Poison Glen*, The Gallery Press (2021). She is a recipient of The Next Generation Artist Award from the Arts of Ireland and a co-recipient of The Markievicz Award. For more information visit www.studiotwentyfive.com.

THINGS I KNOW ABOUT MY FATHER

Annemarie Ní Churreáin

i

On the morning of Annie's funeral I'm the only passenger
boarding a bus from Dublin to Derry City. It's not yet sun-
rise and when the driver asks if I'm from Donegal, I decide
to sit up front. He launches into a story about a stripper on
his Belfast route *who just last night was standing there in the aisle
and took off her clothes.* I catch him looking back at me in the
rear-view mirror. We go the rest of the journey in silence and
in Derry he does not accept my fare. By the time a taxi deliv-
ers me to the edge of Annie's village, the morning light is no
longer trembling. On the front steps of the church I find my
father standing between my mother and my sister. My sister
chirps: *I told you she'd be here.* Inside the church there are no
free seats and the choir has already begun. All I can see are
shoulders and the backs of heads. The scent of incense is sick-
ening and I think again of the bus driver. The priest opens
the Mass by naming aloud *all the beloved children of the deceased,*

here seated together. My father's name is not said. Why didn't I confront that driver? Why did I stay in my seat? My father gives a signal meaning *we're leaving.* We make our exit and minutes later we are sitting around a hotel table. We order four vegetable soups that come in stainless steel bowls. My father does not know who he is or where he belongs. And I don't know why I say it, but I say: *I blame Annie. It's all her fault.*

ii

Growing up in northwest Donegal, the border with Northern Ireland was, at first, another unknowable thing. Like local legends of giants and saints, or the red streak in a stone said to be the blood of a warrior killed over a cow or a daughter. On one side of the world lay the border, on another lay the black Atlantic, and in-between we turned turf on the hill. We chopped logs. We were often on the dole. We were always looking for work. One winter, my father delivered milk; he drove the truck and ticked the list as I ran door to the door in the dark. The following winter, he worked in London. The Christmas we could not afford a tree, he brought his chain-saw into the forest and got chased by a ranger. When he got home, the tree sticking out of the back of the car, he was almost sick with excitement. We had a dog that slept in a rusted barrel toppled sideways and twice a year we scooped the pups out from under her belly and popped them in a bag. My father had a saying: *in this life, the only thing you have to do is die.* I have a distinct memory of my father standing up and of Mary, the woman I knew as my paternal grandmother, sitting down, and my father yelling *Did you think I'd never find out?*

iii

An early memory; If it is a boy, my mother wants to call the new baby *Cormac.* If it's a boy my father wants to give the baby his name. My father slams his fist on the table and the cutlery bounces. My mother, heavy in a smocked dress, gets up slowly from her chair, walks to the kitchen, and takes down a Derry phone number scrawled on a piece of paper that has been pinned to the wall now for several months. My father looks on, incredulous. She dials whilst watching him. She waits. *Hello, is this Annie?* She extends the receiver to my father. The chord will only reach so far. He rises and takes the receiver in both hands. He says: *You probably don't know who I am.*

iv

The border is another unknowable thing and yet, it some-how lives with us, lives in us. And the new, 'real' family are on the other side.

v

Would I like to share my parents? Would I like to give a child a home? It's a warm balmy summer and F, who wears a string of pearls and always kneels when she's talking to children, brings a three-day old baby and passes it carefully, like a blanket of water, to my mother. This is what fostering means. My father is smitten by the baby girl, who cannot stay because she's *pre-adoption*. When the birth mother comes to sign the final papers, she is wearing a pink dress with red roses. She is, maybe, fifteen years old. She stands very far away from the baby. All these years later, the image is still clear in my head; the girl who came to sign the papers; the baby who was about to be signed away. When the paperwork is done, after about six weeks, my mother brings the baby to the family access centre. My father packs away the milk bottles, the soothers, the pram. We put everything in the attic and close the trap door behind us. And for a long time, when we are driving out the Derry road, nobody points anymore to F's house to say jokingly *that's where our baby came from!*

vi

Big Bertha, Miss America, Little Miss Crab. My father had nicknames for anyone who hurt him or scared him. He liked to jest with the Irish language student girls that he'd shoot any boys who came near the house. But on the night of my prom, when my mother broke down crying over my tight, peach dress, he said *Don't mind your mother. She had it rough.* I remember my parents nose to nose in the living room. I remember Patsy Cline on the record player singing

'Three Cigarettes in an Ashtray'. I remember doors slamming (my father in a rage, because I was giving him cheek; my father in a rage because I was too spoiled). Often, he left in the car and was never coming back. He punched a hole in the top of the washing machine and my mother slid a plastic, diamond coloured table mat over the top. He went to mass every Sunday but would not accept communion. My mother kept her old school books in the attic with my father's name and her name inside a red ink heart. In several places her heart is almost bursting through the page. I was obsessed with their wedding album; the oval, flawless face of my mother; the comically serious face of my father with auburn side-burns and a moustache. In one photograph the newly married couple are standing in the bright December sunlight outside the chapel, and lined up behind them in a row – along the steps – are both sets of families; Mary in a smart, tweed suit wearing her brown-rimmed glasses and holding on to her hand-bag as if it is about to be stolen.

vii

Once, drying dishes in an Aunt O's kitchen, the conversation turned to my aunt's friends who had adopted a child from a country abroad. Anxiety, anger issues, attachment disorder: the list of the boy's problems seemed endless to her. Returning a plate into a cupboard, and closing the pine door, she said: *I just don't know why they don't send him back.*

viii

How to tell the difference between what I know, and what my father knows? My father remembers that when he was a teenager he attended a Saturday night dance in a hall by the river near the border. He remembers seeing two identical girls looking at him from across the floor. When, as an adult, he met his twin sisters for the first time, he was able to recall them. In the first photograph I saw of these new sisters, they are pictured in the back of a wedding car, in matching white wedding dresses with matching wide-brimmed floppy white hats. At some stage I was sent into Derry to get to know my cousins. All the boy-cousins looked like my brothers. All the girl cousins looked like me. Annie was the shadow of my father, the same thin lips, the same thread veins in her cheeks. It always seemed to me that Annie's heart was spilling out through her eyes. It ways seemed to me like I did not belong. I walked up a road one day in the drizzling rain and found a phone-box. I called my parents and pleaded *please I want to come home.*

ix

A memory that I thought was lost: It is the occasion of a funeral and I notice the dead man's son, walking behind the coffin. He is in a black leather jacket (unzipped), and has blond hair and blue fishes in his eyes. I am around eighteen years old. Outside the church I am told that the dead man never met the woman who gave birth to him. The dead man's son became my first boyfriend and we lived together for three years, although the relationship was, for two of those years, quite bad. *Why didn't I confront that driver? Why did I stay in my seat?* The first words I ever said to this boyfriend were: *I'm sorry for your loss.*

x

The border has been in my father forever. On the night of my christening, Aunt O recalls that punches were thrown. If I was cheeking him, my father sometimes said *I'll beat the bad thing out of you.* Once he hit me at the dinner table of an elder relative because I was slurping soup and the relative said: *please, not on the head.* He turfed a house-guest out on his ear and threatened to kill him. My father wound up in a shouting match with the neighbour, that almost came to blows, about whose son was definitely not gay. He did not speak to Aunt O for ten years. As I got older he liked to say to me: *well you would know, you went to college. You with your education.* One Father's Day I offered to cook a special meal, and he became upset. He did not understand an invitation, he thought it was a request. If in doubt, my father always said *No.* He did not want me using my laptop in the house. He did not like people going for walks unless he knew where they were going. He installed an electronic locking system on his bedroom door and cameras outside the house. He refused to speak to his teenage foster daughter for several weeks and when I intervened, suggesting that he of all people might he understand *her situation,* he asked me *Who do you think you are? Do you know who you are?* I sat on a bed with my head in my hands, and my mother came in and said what she always said, *you have to let your father think that he's in control.* When I was twenty-three years old, I packed a ruck-sack. Just before I caught the airport bus, his parting words: *don't expect me to pay for the funeral, if you have to be brought back.*

xi

When he first realised that he was ill, my father did not go to the doctor. In fact, he told no-one. A trip had already been planned and for three weeks he drove across a foreign country in the suffocating heat. Did he keep any log of his symptoms? Did he say to himself: *the only thing you have to do in this life is die?* Shortly after coming home, he was diagnosed. Between the chemo treatments, he was angry at everyone, and me in particular. *You're just like Annie. You don't care if I die.* I did not go to my college graduation. In the hospital he wanted water. He could not breathe. I spoke with my sister in the corridor who spoke with a cousin in Derry and asked if Annie might come to see him or, perhaps the plan was to try and bring him to see her. The reply that came back was simply *No.* Even

256

as the colour began to come back into his face, his eyes becoming his eyes again, I knew that something between my father and I had reached a conclusion. When he got home, he did not know what to do with himself. He bought a fishing boat that rarely saw the lake. He installed two horses in a field that out-ran him. He set up a polytunnel in the back yard and began to grow vegetables. I looked out the kitchen window one afternoon and the polytunnel was gone. A gust of wind came, he said, during a bad storm. *And I just let it go.*

xii

A memory of my first driving lesson: my father, in the passenger seat, grips the handle on the roof above his head and instructs me at the wheel of the car. It is late evening in my seventeenth summer and we are in the northwest Donegal bogs, far from the main road. I stall and start. I stall and start again and take off slowly across a slope. My heart is in my mouth. In the back seat my younger sister is yelling *But what about me?* After a while I swap seats with her. She clicks the seat-belt, drops the handbrake, rams the accelerator and the car lurches forward. The car is driving us. The car is headed for a curve. We are sideways in the air. We are the wrong way up. We are falling, falling. We are upside down in the heather, engine still running. My sister is laughing hysterically. I have glass in my mouth. I wriggle out through the rear window, pushing the car off my hips. When I stand, a silver wheel is whirring. I open the crushed right door and let my sister out. I open the crushed left door and let my father out. We are all bleeding, but everyone is alive. A neighbour, who is first to arrive on the scene, brings us all home to the hill, and my mother who sees us coming – and who has already heard the news – walks outside in an apron, a baby on her hip, and stands in wait, the sunlight at her back. She looks at us with astonishment. *You would leave me here? You would leave me here like this?*

THE OLD GHOSTS

Patrick McCabe was born in Clones, County Monaghan in 1955. His novels include *Carn, The Butcher Boy, Breakfast on Pluto, Heartland*, and most recently, *The Big Yaroo*. He has written extensively for stage and screen. His new novel, *Poguemahone*, is due April 2022, from Unbound.

THE MUFFIN MAN

It is by no means common knowledge that sometime in the late 1950s while touring rural Ireland as a young repertory actor, a considerably intoxicated Harold Pinter had been observed clambering onto a parish hall stage, and boisterously endeavouring to share his talents with 'The Mud and Shamrock Pride of Erin' Ceilidh Band.

Before blithely proceeding to retrieve from his belt the sturdiest of little brass bugles and tootling a bravura rendition from Miles Davis's *Kind of Blue*, succeeded by a fifteen-minute rendition of the tediously obscurantist John Coltrane interpretation of Rodgers & Hammerstein's 'My Favourite Things' while an open-mouthed audience looked on in dazed bewilderment.

!

Pah! snorted Vivian Urquhart, relaxing pressure on the vintage marbled fountain pen, *as if I care what the infuriating braggart did in that miserable wet backwater of a would-be republic*, closing the calf-leather covers of his notebook impatiently. *Confessions of a Retired Librarian* was neatly inscribed in copperplate on the frontispiece.

Mr Urquhart was sitting by the window of Costa Coffee on a drizzly mid-winter's afternoon in 2017. With the foregoing 'funny incident' having taken place, of course, entirely within the confines of his own mind, prompting him to include along with the others a spiky graphite caricature of the brazen hypocrite and consistent ingrate Pinter. Pinter, whose sole admirable enterprise, as far as Vivian was concerned, had been his involvement in *The Quiller Memorandum*, which – given the script's willing embrace of opacity and blatant disregard for the imperatives of plausibility – might be said to have a considerable amount in common with the current narrative.

The banal truth being that the Nobel-scooping playwright had never, at any time, been seen to combine with any agglomeration of bumpkin amateur musicians, whether in Ireland or anywhere else. Any more than the chronicler in question, irrespective of his earnest insistence to the contrary, had enjoyed over the years a quite excellent relationship with the playwright's 'incomparably smarter' brother Leonard 'Percy' Pinter. With whom Mr Urquhart had shared – or so he claimed – many pleasant hours engaged in games of chess, prior to Leonard's departure overseas with the services. 'Unstintingly loyal to both Albion and his queen,' Mr Urquhart could often be overheard remarking, 'unlike that other bugle-blowing communist with the pugnacious air and oversized spectacles.'

Neither of which were entirely unlike his own, as it happens.

Sometime after he had left the café, he noticed his notebook was missing. He was some way down the road and was about to turn back for it, when he heard a voice.

'You look a little like Eric Morecambe.' It was the waitress, pursuing him with his notebook in hand. 'You left this behind, Sir!' Without so much as a hint of shame confiding that she had, in fact, been casually perusing the material therein.

'None of this could possibly be true,' she had commented, as he gratefully accepted the bound volume from her hands. 'Could it?'

'Tell me honestly, do you see before you anything other than a tired old librarian?' he replied.

'You seem a little pale, Mr Urquhart. Perhaps this past few days, you've been feeling poorly?'

He shook his head.

'Well, all I can say is – going by this – you certainly have a vivid imagination!' the waitress laughed, gratifying him by not taking a tip.

There may be some hope for us yet, he thought, crossing the road in the pelting rain; somewhat relieved and uplifted by the young lady's old-fashioned credulousness. *Happily, on this occasion, no pressing need to confuse, deny or disrupt*, he pondered, folding his umbrella as he disappeared inside the house.

*

It may have been his wayward musings upon the already referenced theatrical presentation *The Quiller Memorandum*, considered Vivian, but whatever the reason, it had occurred to him while squatting anonymously by his appointed window that with his Alec Guinness overcoat and strikingly diffident manner, he might reasonably have emerged from the pages of any number of paperback 'spy stories' – the type which, of late, he had begun reading to his nephew Jason; a live-in resident of Haberdashers' Aske's Academy, Crayford.

'I really do so love thrillers,' his nephew had robustly declared. 'And the manner in which you deliver them is nothing short of magisterial, if you don't mind me saying so.'

Vivian Urquhart had smiled – a tad faintly, he recalled – continuing with his bedside performance; a selected excerpt from the *Inheritance of Treason*.

There has always been in England an uncertainty of ambivalence, characterised by a flow of democratic sentiment which pushes against the Britannic ideal. Now in the twenty-first century, it is surely time for such tendencies to be suspended.

With all his resources being required to suppress a small smile when the poster outside The Empire caught his eye:

The Intelligence Men, starring Eric Morecambe.

Featuring his partner Ernie Wise – *the same as myself and Perry, ha ha!* he found himself chuckling – as the unlikeliest pair of state actors imaginable.

*

Vivian Urquhart's nephew received regular monthly visits – during the course of which the boy willingly professed himself an addict of international deceit and intrigue, acknowledging a certain chagrin occasioned by the fact that his uncle, in spite of his avowed affections for a certain Mr Sean Connery over Daniel Craig, at one time had, in fact, been an associate of the internationally renowned author Ian Fleming.

Although to claim he had known him intimately would have been a stretch, Mr Urquhart accepted – having encountered Fleming, at the very most, on three occasions – once at his island retreat and subsequently at the popular *demi-monde* venue where the jazz *chanteuse* Cleo Laine performed regularly on Commercial Road, East London.

Bap-bap-a-doop! she would improvise on the small stage under the spotlight; those long elegant hands fashioning serpentine configurations, a sheath-gowned shadow bathed in speckled blue.

Be under no illusion, dear boy, Fleming had pronounced that evening. *But that the privately-educated Englishman is the greatest and most untrustworthy dissembler on earth. There is no-one who acts braver when he is frightened stiff, or who can flatter you even as he loathes your very being ... and that of your country, for that matter.*

Such an eclectic clientele as the old Nucleus Club attracted in those days, mused Vivian. Vagabonds ranging from the neurotic sound engineer to that of Urquhart's most valued associate and former services colleague. For dearest Perry Deakin had also been in the company on that occasion, enjoying a spot of baccarat along with the Caribbean resident and inspired creator of James Bond.

Unlike 'Old 'Arold', Perry had actually been a bona fide prodigy, in every aspect of the arts – as when he had elected to clamber onstage for the purpose of combining with Cleo Laine and the house band. Unlike that communist boor Pinter, Vivian could have listened to him playing all night.

For Perry, he really was quite a dab hand on his 'liquorice-stick' as he called his clarinet. A virtuoso, really – rendering, among others, the tunes of Miles and Thelonius Monk – in Mr Urquhart's view, both by far the best of the bebop 'beret-and-dark glasses boys'. Who, in fact, given Vivian's fondness for swing and old-timers such as Glenn Miller and Benny Goodman, he could only just about tolerate – and did so for Perry's sake.

The mental scribblings of a subnormal child was how he elected to classify those self-indulgent, chromatic presentations favoured by Coltrane and the rest of his degenerate solipsistic crew.

The heart of whoredom was what Perry liked to call the large spacious room of The Nucleus, where the air was so thick with reefer smoke you could just about see your hand in front of your face. Or make out what the former radar station employee Joe Meek might be trying to say, weaving precariously in and out among the tables.

Unless you're reconciled, be assured that the undead will do for you. And I ought to know because I talk to them regular.

*

At that time, neither Vivian's mother nor poor 'Little' Dolly Quinlan had been very long deceased. But, as Joe Meek had suggested:

Do not be distressed, because I know for a fact that your beloved mother, she is not gone, being in existence just beyond the range of our vision. You'll wake up one night and she'll have returned as your guardian angel. I know this because I'm in receipt of certain 'signals'.

Joe Meek's experiments with the otherworld were legendary – not only in his trademark reedy Woolworth's organ effect, but in the speeded-up vocals and rapid percussion accompanied by the sound of a creaking coffin or frighteningly real female scream.

Few in the club had taken him seriously. Not until he had shot his landlady, at any rate, in his digs opposite the graveyard on Holloway Road. Then, subsequently, himself. The landlady had challenged him over his clandestine nocturnal wanderings – not only to the cemetery with his extraordinary freightload of amplifiers, loudspeakers and wires – but to the gentlemen's convenience directly opposite.

The police were here again today, she informed him.

There were rumours that he may have even recorded the murder. For the reels on the tape machine were still running when the police arrived. Relaying what had been described in the papers as a 'wasp's-nest-like' sound – like something eddying from a place we know nothing about.

A buzzing, muted tornado.

And a frightening, female scream.

Such were the 'signals' he had spoken of since boy-hood, when – as an 'indoors' child obsessed with gadgetry in rural Gloucestershire – he had rigged up speakers in local orchards to entertain the cherry-pickers. The same percussion, the same reedy organ. And the coffin lid too. Perhaps the female scream.

*

Vivian Urquhart resided in a four-storey yellow-brick converted home in North London: Number 45 Brondesbury Road.

Where of late, he sighed ruefully, he had not been sleeping at all well.

Just the slightest creak of a floorboard was more than enough to alert him to the recollection of a girl's naked body lying prostrate at the foot of a sloping stone bank, on the foreshore somewhere in East London. Face down, head pointing upriver.

Compared to what had happened to Little Quinlan, his mother's aneurism appeared to him now as nothing.

How he bitterly regretted ever going near that woman.

Having been alerted early on to Little Quinlan's status as a part-time 'mystery girl', place of residence unknown.

Don't be an ass, dear boy. Beware the heart of whoredom, please.

He vividly recalled Perry's firm counsel – never, at the time, having dared to dream that already he was sowing the seeds of the destruction of his marriage.

He had literally fallen upon Little Dolly Quinlan in The Nucleus. The night of Queen Elizabeth's Coronation as it happened.

At 8.55 a.m. the following morning, the divisional surgeon had arrived in Chiswick – Corney Reach – pronouncing the life of Dolores Quinlan extinct. But then, where's the use of thinking about all that again, he chided himself, turning the page of a favoured, well-thumbed volume entitled *Old Blighty's Shore: from Dan Leno's Theatre Royal to Margaret Thatcher, Years of Growth.*

*

In recent times, Vivian Urquhart had begun to ponder the verisimilitude of Joe Meek's eccentric assertions with regard to the possible existence of 'signals', as he described them.

Hints from another world, injunctions from beyond the grave; which Vivian Urquhart no longer scorned – certainly not in recent times.

This significant modification of attitude had manifested itself most directly in the aftermath of a dread sighting of none other than 'Little' Dolores Quinlan – standing motionless by the window with her hair braided in the French plait style, remaining still; entirely without emotion.

When he looked again, she had vanished without trace, with nothing remaining but the thin, intermittent rattle of a dusty grey Venetian blind.

Still significantly shaken, Vivian remained there on the bed, the back of his shirt entirely soaked.

French plait? he puzzled. *I've never known her to wear such a thing.*

Then he heard the strange but familiar buzzing sound.

Wasps. Or like wasps, suggested by a reedy organ, with the greatest anxiety being that the following night she might return, and if she did that he might not survive.

Just like me, he heard the shuffling figure of Joe Meek murmuring, observing Vivian over the rim of his glasses.

Then, within seconds, he too was gone. No wasp's nest, no gaudy organ. Nothing. Just a vast and all-embracing silence.

*

With the preponderance of Google Earth and Google Glass in these saturated times, Mr Urquhart murmured, in situ by the café window, *we confront an unprecedented blitz of information data and noise.*

He had been labouring assiduously on his memoir since early spring, having commenced with the communist

Pinter's drink-sodden tours of the back roads and grim theatrical shacks of rural Ireland. A geography with which he was more than familiar, of course, due to his intermittent postings as a young man in Ulster.

He had also included among his pages a number of rudimentary sketches – some of his place of residence, along with a number of less than flattering caricatures of its residents.

The ubiquitous navvying Irishman dwelt, appropriately, in the basement of No. 45, with a family of Hindustanis occupying two of the larger rooms upstairs. On the top floor resided a same sex couple – a Polish dancer and her so-called lover. In the evenings you could hear the wild, energetic strains of Stravinsky as her rehearsal of *The Firebird* scaled to its crescendo; by all accounts Dyta Zelenski had a production of this 'infernal dance' pending in the world-famous Sadler's Wells theatre.

At this point, he was concluding his final paragraph about Dolores. How wrenching that morning trip to Chiswick had been. If only it had been possible for his wife Beatrice to forgive him; though few spouses locate such fortitude within themselves. Especially considering what Dolly Quinlan had done: Called to their suburban house one evening, hopelessly intoxicated, waving that skinny little fist as she hurled yet another flurry of contemptible expletives.

He had pleaded incessantly with Beatrice, but to no avail.

And thus it had ended, all because of some low-bred Irish skivvy.

But then that was the way of such people, he sighed. As with veal, dispiritingly unreliable.

Failing Perry Deakin's characteristically unperturbed corroboration to the investigating officers, he shuddered to think what might have transpired.

Dear Perry, he whispered softly. *One's eternal gratitude will remain exclusively yours.*

He smiled and decided to cheer himself up by treating himself to yet another tasty muffin; a brand also favoured by his long-term section colleague.

We are The Muffin Men, Perry used to render on the clarinet. *Who live on Drury Lane.*

The confections were of the blueberry variety, generally freshly-baked.

For just a brief moment the slightest of chills went coursing through him, when he considered the sheer enormity of the task which he had only recently assigned to himself. Because now, as he realised, he was in fact approaching 'the appointed time.'

Before long he found himself, dazedly, crossing the street on his way back to 45 Brondesbury Road. To his astonishment, erupting into laughter as he stood on the front step, awkwardly twisting the front door key – having sworn that he'd apprehended a certain dark-suited figure standing behind him – Joe Meek regarded him closely over the rim of his glasses.

Remaining here, pale and formal, exhibiting the stiff implacability of what, to all intents and purposes, appeared that of a living corpse – transporting Vivian to those familiar, brooding wet lanes of miserable Mid-Ulster – and, specifically, the occasion of their abduction of the dairy-farmer Ginger Cochrane. *Silly bugger. Ought not to have been there*, complained Vivian Urquhart, trembling violently all of a sudden.

What is that you have in your hand? he heard Joe Meek inquiring softly, his fingers gliding through that Brylcreemed quiff. *It wouldn't by any chance be a box of matches? Embarking, perhaps, Vivian – are you – on an unspoken private operation? A small insurgency of your own, perhaps? Because if it is, rest assured that I shall be on hand to provide you with whatever assistance might be required. A wasp's nest perhaps – even a little scream?*

Vivian Urquhart slid the thin yellow cardboard box open, meticulously extracting from the interior a single splint, sharply pinching its head between finger and thumb.

I saw the Mau Mau last night, he heard Joe Meek sigh. *In the graveyard, out among the stones. They were wielding cricket bats.*

Do you like muffins? replied Mr Urquhart. *Perry and I, we're fools for them, really.*

He twinkled just a little, lowering his head as he hummed along:

Do you know the muffin man
the muffin man, the muffin man
do you know the muffin man

who lives on Drury Lane?

His visitor, however, had already departed.

What a liability old Perry could be at times, thought Vivian. *Especially in his cups.* So indiscreet.

The pipes over in Notting Hill are stuffed to buggery with the half-born brats of our Commonwealth friends, and the drains are no better than they should be!

Anyone, for heaven's sake, could have been listening. The indiscreet old devil. But that, of course, was all history now – ever since Perry had renounced his former career.

I find these days that I'm world-weary, to be honest, he had confided in Vivian. *It's all just a lot of shit now; certainly after Suez. All Albion has been doing since then is playing silly games, my friend.*

Hmm, mused Urquhart. *We'll soon see about that.*

Taking his time, he assembled the white Swan Vesta splints in a row, simultaneously giving his attention to the highlights of the Nottingham test match issuing through the baize of the ancient Pye radio, bequeathed to him by his father.

Quislings, he snapped suddenly. *Collaborators every one!*

He flicked his thumb as a golden spark flared.

Which is why I have been left with no choice.

Naming each country, he removed the individual matches, one by one like a small terrace forming. How beautiful it looked, elevating the blue-bonneted flare before bending over and applying it lovingly to the edge of the curtain.

krrk

crackle

whumph!

Is that the ghost of a reedy organ I hear?

No, he decided. But of course it's not.

As usual, it's just my imagination, he sighed, coughing ever so slightly as he gently closed the apartment door behind him. There wasn't so much as a sound in the building, with everyone having departed for the bank holiday weekend.

Just in that instant, however, Vivian Urquhart could have sworn that he'd heard a creaking sound – perhaps that of a creaking floorboard.

Might it just be possible that there was someone in the attic?

*

Once outside, he hailed a passing taxi. A black cab thankfully, and not one of those odious rustbuckets piloted by some dour illiterate as off they sped in the direction of Paddington Station.

At last, my friend, today's the day! he announced to the driver, smartly tapping the glass partition. *Very soon we'll be shot of them all!*

You mean the European vote? I didn't think they'd actually go through with it, to be honest.

Mr Urquhart acknowledged privately that it was his genuine hope that there had been no-one else present in the house, in the attic or anywhere else. Especially not Dyta Zelenski, whose artistry, in spite of everything, one could not help but admire.

How ironic it would be – should he have actually perpetrated an error of such appalling magnitude – to witness her writhing, executing yet another 'infernal dance'.

And Joe Meek, perhaps, laughing.

Needing the occasion to justify my female scream.

Vivian had personally encountered the Polish dancer on but two occasions, and would never forget her breath-taking impertinence. With her arms folded, the very essence of ingratitude. Complaining of Mr Urquhart's late night predilection for playing jazz – or 'tiddly-bop' as Miss Zelenski from Gdansk on the Baltic coast preferred.

Tiddly-bop indeed, thought Vivian Urquhart, wincing.

In actual fact, he loathed Miles Davis, Coltrane or any of the rest of them.

As a matter of fact, I was playing Benny Goodman, he explained.

Which, of course, meant nothing to Miss Baltic Sea, who had flounced off brazenly with the oriental dressing gown flapping insubordinately behind her.

Must you have please to see it! he heard her calling back.

Whatever that was supposed to mean. When he heard her words, he had, in actual fact, felt sick.

It's just like Ulster all over again, he said to himself. *Cochrane and his Border-hopping murderers, not language at all.*

But enough of that, thought Mr Urquhart, as the cab pulled up at Paddington Station. And very shortly he was billeted in a warm train compartment en route to The Walpole Hotel and the bracing seaside resort of Cliftonville Bay.

John Edrich was an excellent opening batsman who could always have beaten out any Kenyan's bowling, Vivian contended privately, while standing at the front desk accepting his room key and pursuing the genial porter who had offered to accompany him to the fifth floor along with his luggage.

Except that it wasn't the fifth floor – just as it transpired that the porter wasn't in fact that either, but someone with the substance of one of Joe Meek's cemetery signals, amounting to little more than a silhouette standing by his side.

The truth was that Vivian Urquhart didn't feel at all well, and looking in the mirror, what he saw reflected back at him was a figure appraising him in its turn – running a finger along a slender black tie with eyes dilated, face powder-white.

Bzz, said Joe. *You'll have to wait for the female scream.* His lips parted thinly as he started to laugh.

The sham-porter had by now departed, succeeded in Vivian's mind by a steady, ordered procession of faces.

The comedian Tommy Trinder he immediately recognised.

What with all them muffins you been eating lately, he heard Tommy bleat. *I think you ought to set up in Drury Lane!*

Where all your secrets can singsong-dance in a circle with the dead, smiled Dan Leno as he wandered past. *In the gaslight like they did when I was in the world.*

Also appearing were Bud Flanagan, George Formby and an old favourite, *The Clitheroe Kid*.

Who had expired on the morning of his own mother's funeral.

Another suicide, just like Joe Meek.

Tsk tsk tsk.

His head began spinning.

Shut your presumptive, imperial mouth! You and yours, they didn't even give me a chance. Because they hate the likes of me, anything got to do with the imagination. Thinking you know what's best for us, but you don't. Neither you nor Perry, damn you!

You don't! snapped Meek, grabbing him roughly and placing him in a headlock.

Then, within a matter of seconds, he was gone.

He's right, suggested a muffled voice from the corner. *That fellow with the dark glasses. He's right you know.*

With the utterance turning out to be that of Cochrane, the Armagh farmer, slowly emerging from the shadows.

You and that Ampleforth Captain lifted me that night in the farmyard. Tell me this, now that sufficient time has passed, and apparently we have peace in our country – was it absolutely necessary to apply the pliers to my nails, like you did?

You're delusional, man. All my life I have never been anything other than a simple librarian.

Sure! snarled Cochrane. *But of course you have!* Exhibiting that sullen, hooded expression for which his sort were historically renowned: the defiant sunken eyes, the uncooperative downturned mouth.

The weight of imagined grievance, thought Mr Urquhart. About as valid as all the other charges routinely directed towards myself and Perry, prompted by our unswerving allegiance to Albion.

The unconscious cruelty and calculating taciturnity.

He had heard it all before.

Your country right or wrong! spat the curly ginger felon.

Then, just as dramatically as Meek, once again he was gone.

Thank heavens for that, Mr Urquhart groaned.

As he checked his watch, he permitted himself the tiniest sip of soda water. There would be ample time for alcohol later.

When Perry, as had been arranged, called up from reception.

Ho hum, late again, murmured Vivian irritably. Because in this regard his former associate never failed to disappoint.

Vivian stood for a moment by the window. How beautiful the south coast looked, he thought. Just like the blue remembered hills of his childhood.

And then sat down to wait, with eyes firmly fixed on the telephone by the bedside.

He got up.

He sat down.

He seemed quite unaware that he was obsessively wringing his hands, nonetheless assured that this time he was going to give Perry the solid chessboard trouncing that his old comrade so richly deserved. The humbling truth, in fact, was that his former colleague had annihilated him on no less than three occasions. Ever since their annual meetings had begun.

He actually felt like sobbing at this point – committing himself to a sustained bout of unrestrained weeping – such was the degree of elation he had begun experiencing. Even as he acknowledged that there were those who might resent his recent accomplishment: or *The Queen's Park Resolution*, as he now tended to think of it. Because, after all, few nations treasured the primacy of private property more than his own. And Number 45 Brondesbury Road had recently been valued at over three million pounds.

However, considerable benefit would derive from his resoluteness, he felt certain, wincing slightly as he remained by the window, experiencing a fleeting pleasure as the light over Thanet gradually began thinning' directing his gaze once more towards the obstinately silent instrument at his bedside.

Nothing.

A full hour was yet to pass in silence.

Then, with a shocking abruptness, he could have sworn he heard his name being spoken, followed by the sound of rhythmic, even breathing. The name 'Joe Meek' returned starkly to his mind. But when he flung the louvred doors of the closet open, there was nothing but the tinkling of slender, shadowed wire hangers.

He assumed his place by the window once more, staring fixedly at the phone.

Still mute.

He could have sworn he had definitely seen a shape, slowly drifting past the curtain.

Which he then excitedly tore from its fittings.

To, again, find nothing. No Joe Meek, nor 'signals' of any kind: just a semi-open window admitting the faintest gust of breeze.

Balling the grey-white gauze material in his lap, Mr Urquhart wilted under a surging wave of shame.

Then, as beads of perspiration began lining up on his forehead, he heard the whisper of his nephew's voice.

Read me The Inheritance of Reason, *Uncle. Will you? Please say you will.*

Vivian Urquhart stood up and struck the wall violently.

It's not reason, it's treason! *Reason has got nothing to do with it, Jason!* he rasped. *Because this is Albion, or don't you understand? What on earth is wrong with everyone?*

There was nothing for it but to call reception.

He raised the receiver to his ear.

Appearing to the operator to be really in quite a state.

How do I get a line out? he repeated.

Before, to his complete surprise, finding himself conversing not with some scarcely interested, immature telephonist, but his former wife, Beatrice Swann.

Thirty years they had been together.

His mother, of course, had warned him about her.

Make a point of avoiding tiny women, she had cautioned. *For I have observed in them grave tendencies, son, which alarm me. They are inclined to bully, in all likelihood to compensate for what they lack in stature, becoming endowed with a sense of their own superiority. Also*, she had added, *they are inclined to talk too much.*

All of which had certainly been true of Bea.

As a matter of fact, he remembered, there were times when Swann ... she would never shut up. The only occasion, however, that he had ever witnessed her being properly, *furiously* angry was when he had neglected to sufficiently shake the earth from a tuft of freshly uprooted grass.

An egregious way of weeding! she had snapped without warning, resulting in a response which Vivian would forever regret. Because, up until then, he had never so much as laid a finger on her person, never mind bodily strike her.

It had distressed him considerably for months on end, requiring as it did all of his resources to conceal her place of interment underneath the patio from both public view and that of his experienced, ever-vigilant superiors. A likely story, it might be said, the sick daydreams of a mild-mannered civil servant. Except that it was true, as there she lay, in the shade of the overhanging linden she so loved.

Poor Bea, he sobbed.

However, in spite of her legendary finickiness and impatience, she had always been someone with whom you could share a laugh. That unique tinkle, as he thought of it. The way she doubled up, with her bundle of knitting still resting in her lap.

Whenever he had encountered the lovely Beatrice Swann first, the character she had suggested more than any other was that of Laura, played by Celia Johnson, in Noël Coward's celebrated *Brief Encounter*.

How Bea could dramatise that entertaining story, with her eyes crinkling up at the corners as she surrendered helplessly to its suppressed passions.

Oh that Donald Duck, he really does make me laugh, you know. His dreadful energy and those blind, exasperated rages!

But what could possibly be wrong with her now? he wondered, with the earpiece still pressing hard against his temple.

Listen to me, dear. Perry Deakin is dead. He passed ten years ago. Don't you remember going to his funeral?

And at that point Vivian Urquhart summoned all of his resolve; that formidable tenacity which rarely failed him in times of necessity.

Dead, you say? How remiss of me. I was so looking forward to celebrating the success of Brexit with a number of small libations in the lounge. As soon as we've concluded our little chess tournament.

Celebrating Brexit? he heard the lovely Beatrice respond. *But didn't you hear? It's been abandoned again. The announcement was made in all the papers.*

With the instrument then, limply, falling from his grasp as the entire room began filling up with wasps. And a certain record producer appeared dramatically once again, leaning insouciantly against the jamb of the bathroom door, sliding his fingers through his gleaming pompadour as he coolly regarded those elegantly manicured fingernails.

At least, I suppose, there wasn't a female scream.

By now Vivian Urquhart was at his wits' end.

Is everything all right? he then heard the porter whisper sympathetically. *When you didn't answer I let myself in.*

He'd been pressing the door buzzer for ages, the uniformed young man explained apologetically.

As Mr Urquhart gazed down at the hopelessly shredded pillow.

Foam, of course, he nodded, not feathers. Yet another nonsensical regulation, no doubt.

Looking up and realising that all about him was quiet once more, the considerate porter having effected his departure.

*

It was late that evening when Vivian Urquhart finally arrived home to Queen's Park, only to find Costa Coffee resolutely barred and shuttered.

Not to worry, he smiled, searching anxiously for his trusty brown paper bag and, to his relief, locating it safe and secure.

With the confusion along Brondesbury Road now, at long last, beginning to show signs of dissipation, the flames, more or less, began petering out. Observing proceedings from across the street, Mr Urquhart noted a cracked yellow table lamp of his own, tilted abjectly on its side as the very last of the onlookers dispersed. They said the blaze had been raging all day.

Dyta, oh poor Dyta, he overheard someone lament.

The staircase had completely collapsed, by all accounts, with the result being that she'd been trapped in the attic the whole afternoon.

It was just by the grace of God she'd survived.

Her companion, lover – or however they preferred to describe themselves these days – appeared to be quite inconsolable, led away under a heavy woollen blanket.

Yet another blackened beam swung dangerously onto the street, and a lone winding tendril rose up from a yawning lattice, elegant as the arm of a dancer.

Am I haunted? Vivian Urquhart wondered.

*

I don't really know, he heard himself moan. For which of us knows the precise nature of things?

He was reflecting on an article he had read earlier in the *London Evening Standard*, which he had snipped out and inserted into his notebook, detailing an episode on the Tube where two city bankers had, unaccountably, set about one another, beating each other preposterously with umbrellas, to the accompanying sound of *Leave!* and *Remain!* in a performance which, without doubt, would have made 'that old 'Arold' green with envy.

!!

Not 'arf, tee hee!, chuckled Mr Urquhart.

Shaking his head in the contented afterglow of his achievement (there would be consequences, of course, but those could be confronted later on) before eventually turning in the direction of Edgware Road, where a Sky News screenshot ever so briefly caught his eye.

Renewed Brexit Fears, had the effect of tickling him pink.

After all, having done his bit, what more could possibly be asked of him?

Bap-ba-ba-ba-doop, he continued, striding on towards Maida Vale; improvising as Cleo might have in Ronnie Scott's or The Nucleus.

Bap-ba-ba-doop they can't say I've not done my bit!

He perambulated for many hours as he considered the events of the day, before finally arriving in Charing Cross Road just as it began to rain, standing in the breaking dawn beneath the drizzle, now waiting for the doors of Ray's Jazz Shop & Café to open; there to remain by the window, and patiently observe the world going by.

Returning to the final draft of his memoir, dreaming of Joe Meek moving noiselessly among the stones, recording Dolly Quinlan's thin, ever-weakening cries. And remembering how she had rested her sweet little tight-permed head, so unguardedly, against his chest, on that glorious night of Queen Elizabeth's Coronation.

Anatomising history, as is my wont, he wrote. *Events both immediate and far removed, but with a recall rather impressive for someone whose mental faculties are, purportedly, gravely imperilled. I mean,* cortical atrophy – *honestly, Dr Khan, I've never heard such piffle in my life. You can count yourself lucky that old Perry's not still around, for we'd put a stop to your so-called Alzheimer's Clinic. Ooh, I say! Those look like a nice tasty set of buns! Waitress, my love, might I trouble you for another?*

Sighing approvingly as he nibbled on a warm fresh muffin; majestically alone, the way Mr Urquhart had always liked it best.

Colette Bryce has published five poetry collections with Picador. *The Whole & Rain-domed Universe* (2014), which draws on her experience of growing up in Derry during the Troubles, received a Ewart-Biggs Award in memory of Seamus Heaney. *Selected Poems* (2017) was winner of the Pigott Prize for Irish poetry. She is the current editor of *Poetry Ireland Review*.

HELICOPTERS

Over time, you picture them
after dark, in searches

focusing on streets and houses
close above the churches

or balancing
on narrow wands of light.

And find so much depends upon
the way you choose

to look at them:
high in the night

their minor flares confused
among the stars, there –

almost beautiful.
Or from way back

over the map
from where they might resemble

a business of flies
around the head-wound of an animal.

DON'T SPEAK TO THE BRITS, JUST PRETEND THEY DON'T EXIST

Two rubber bullets stand on the shelf,
from Bloody Sunday – mounted in silver,

space rockets docked and ready to go off;
like the Sky Ray Lolly that crimsons your lips

when the orange Quencher your brother gets
attracts a wasp that stings him on the tongue.

'Tongue' is what they call the Irish language,
'native tongue' you're learning at school.

Kathleen is sent home from the Gaeltacht
for speaking English, and it's there

at the Gaeltacht, ambling back
along country roads in pure darkness

that a boy from Dublin
talks his tongue right into your mouth,

holds you closely in the dark and calls it
French kissing (he says this in English).

A SPIDER

I trapped a spider in a glass,
a fine-blown wineglass.
It shut around him, silently.
He stood still, a small wheel
of intricate suspension, cap
at the hub of his eight spokes,
inked eyes on stalks; alert,
sensing a difference.
I meant to let him go
but still he taps against the glass
all Marcel Marceau
in *the wall that is there but not there,*
a circumstance I know.

NORTH TO THE SOUTH

1

The map unfolded in the car
like a kite, a barely
controllable thing
to be wrestled, my father
overcome.

A giant's hands
might have practised origami,
a bird, or a boat
on which an impossible dream
might stay afloat.

2

A head through the window
on the driver's side.

Where have we come from?
Where are we going?

Eight little girls and a dog
spill out.

Aunty Máire was famous
for spelling out her name

P-Ó-G M-O T-H-Ó-I-N,
which they duly wrote down.

3

You are giving the vast Atlantic
to your father, bucketful
by bucketful, padding

to and fro on the damp strand
to store it at his feet
in a hole where

it only appears to vanish.

WHEN I LAND IN NORTHERN IRELAND

When I land in Northern Ireland I long for cigarettes,
for the blue plume of smoke hitting the lung with a thud
    and, God,
the quickening blood as the stream administers the nicotine.
Stratus shadows darkening the crops
when coming in to land,
coming in to land.

What's your poison?
A question in a bar
draws me down through a tunnel of years
to a time preserved in a cube of fumes, the seventies-
    yellowing
walls of remembrance; everyone smokes and talks about
    the land,
the talk about the land, our spoiled inheritance.

HERITANCE

From her? Resilience. Generosity.
A teacher's gravitas.
Irish stew. A sense
of the ridiculous. High ceilings.
Neither a borrower nor a lender be.
Operatic plotlines.
Privacy.

An artery leading to the Spanish Armada,
a galleon dashed on the rocks at Moville, a sunken
grave, *se llama Hernando,*
black hair, despair,
a rose between the teeth.
Bullets. Books.
A low-toned voice.

An Antarctic explorer in a fur-lined hood
with the face of a pugilist
and a Russian wife in Brooklyn.
Bottles, half-full,
tilting in the ottoman.
O rhesus negative.
Tact, to a point.

Uncle Joe walking out of the Dáil in '22,
sold down the river.
An historical anger.
Stand-up piano.
Pilgrim feet.
A comic turn of phrase.
An iron constitution.

THE REPUBLICANS

Their walls are like any other walls, muffled in layers of
    paste and paper.
Squares compete with a carpet's swirls. The room is
    a-clutter with adolescents,
children, ashtrays, dirty cups; a television's flash and jabber.

A man reclines in an armchair, dragged up close to the
    hearth, his feet
on the shelf. Glowing coals are banked with slack.
    Cooking smells waft in
from beyond the door. Two schoolgirls braid each other's hair.

Jesus opens his ruptured chest in a frame; in another,
    Jesus again
at an earlier age, in his mother's arms. In a third, a
    triptych in household gloss
depicts a map, a gun, and a dove. *Ireland unfree shall never
    be at peace*

spelled out by sons in prison workshops. The republicans
rest their plates on their knees and gobble up their
    dinners, quickly.
Mince. Potatoes. Peas or beans. They light their fags and
    inhale, deeply.

299

Conor O'Callaghan was born in Newry and grew up in Dundalk. He has published five collections of poems, one memoir and two novels. His most recent books are *Live Streaming*, Gallery Press (2017) and *We Are Not in the World*, Doubleday (2021).

THE DUCK

The Duck came up the Quay's south shore three times a day during high season, more on weekends. You heard it before you saw it. An antiquated mechanical growl come clattering out of the blue from the north. Then the thing itself, like an alien spaceship from the films, materialised through our vanishing point.

The Duck, says Dad.

We would be sitting in deckchairs out the front when our father said that. He would say that looking out to sea through German field-glasses. There was this little patch of lawn before our converted wooden train carriage, overlooking the Quay's south shore. On a good day you can see to Dublin. So much of those summers, from June to the first week of September, mid-afternoon to teatime, were spent thus: in our little patch of garden, watching the evening traffic through a pair of German field-glasses fetched from one of several bodies that me and our Finny had trawled ashore.

The Duck, says I.

The War was not long over. We had been neutral throughout. But the Quay is only three miles south of the narrow mouth of Carlingford Lough. That was the peculiar thing. For six years, the War was the other side of that narrow mouth. We could hear the War, and sometimes we could see it as well. Wreckage from sunk vessels, the wing of a spitfire, even the cluster of gulls in the offing that announced another body washing ashore.

The last flotsam of War was The Duck.

On the opposite shore heading south is this proper seaside village called the Rock. On the Rock's front was a shop owned by Donny O'Shea. Donny sold shillelaghs and dolls with oversized heads in cellophane coated with dust. The same Donny was owed big dollars from running cigarettes to the Air Force base in Greencastle, our father said. When no cash was forthcoming, Donny accepted payment in kind in the form of an amphibious landing craft salvaged off Omaha Beach. On both flanks was stencilled: **DUKW US MARINE CORPS**. Hence 'The Duck'.

Donny ran jollies on The Duck. The Duck departed the Rock thrice daily: north to Greencastle to pooch around the derelict base and maybe walk the length of the runway for the B52s, then stop off on the way back at the Quay.

On hot weekends in high season, The Duck would be crammed to the gills with day-trippers. Twenty-four at a time. All upright in their frocks and woollen jackets, laughing, like marines going to their eternal reward. The Duck climbed up our strand. Bathers parted while it did. The Duck climbed far enough for its end to clear the tidemark and footwear not get soaked. Its flap creaked down.

The trippers all jumped off and stood around and laughed some more. Some bought ninety-nines. Some drank fast pints out the front of McCrystals' shorefront alehouse. Twenty minutes of that. The trippers all climbed back aboard, and The Duck growled off, into hazy silence between here and the Rock.

Donny made massive money out of it, far more than was owed to him.

Until the following came to pass.

One fifteenth of August in the late forties was a Sunday. Nineteen hundred and forty-eight? Somewhere there. Fifteenth of August is the blessing of the shrines. All the farmers of Monaghan and Armagh descended upon the Rock. They packed the boarding houses. Their huge paws made pint glasses resemble thimbles. They walked the prom in suit-pants held upright with braces or twine or both, eating two cones at once. There would be chair-o-planes, a waltzer, a tug-o-war if the tide was out.

That Sunday that happened to be the fifteenth of August, The Duck made no fewer than five round-trips. Clear and hot all day. The last of those must have been gone eight o'clock. We had our tea well finished.

The Duck, says Dad.

The Duck, says I.

Back again, says Dad. Somebody's making a pretty shilling.

The Duck had taken some stick. It was clattering like the hammers. It was leaving big gulps of diesel in its

303

wake. It pulled up the strand and there climbed down two dozen of the rarest country men. Nicely with porter. Dad handed over the field-glasses. I could see the country men as if they were at the end of our garden. Battered fedoras and suits worn shiny from labouring and mismatched blazers and barely a straight tooth between them. Even our Finny stepped out to get a look and persuaded me to descend amongst them.

The sun was big and warm yet, but it was disappearing by the new time. The country men looked lost. Fish out of water. Big jaws and long arms and sunken eyes. They trod on one another's shadows. Their boots left prints in the sand's corrugations. We tried talking to them, men to men. I had just left school, Finny was in his early twenties. To them, we must have looked and sounded like kittens. They spoke words understood only to themselves. They were ghosts, it felt like. They were revenants of a whole other epoch.

Donny came back down from McCrystals', his face flushed, and beckoned all back aboard before the light was lost. A small crowd was gathered to wave them off. They were holding onto the bars overhead where tarp would go. They were laughing amongst themselves.

The Duck wouldn't restart. When the time came, and they were back aboard, The Duck refused to quack. However long they left it. However blue Donny swore.

Come on ya fucker! Donny was shouting. Come the fuck on!

One of the country men launched into 'Goodnight Irene'. The others laughed more and joined him.

Sometimes I live in the country
Sometimes I live in town
Sometimes I have a great notion
To jump in the river and drown

Donny demanded quietness midway through the first chorus. Donny O'Shea had hair a black not found in nature and big flyaway collars and a shirt invariably unbuttoned to the naval and skin as tanned as leather. Donny seemed convinced that there was some connection between their singing and The Duck's ailing mechanicals. The starter motor was making a frightful grating. After a fashion, it made nothing.

Donny went up to ring from the coinbox. The country men sat on a breakwater outside McCrystals'. You had the feeling that some were as far from home as they had ever been, and they can't have been very far. We sat with them. Some fishermen stood around as well. Fishermen and farmers do not mix. There was nothing to say almost, no shared ground to speak of. One fisherman aptly-named Tony Sharkey told them all about the War, as if the people of Monaghan and Armagh had not lived through the same. And they duly listened, like they had never heard tell of such wonders.

It was like the War, says Tony pointing behind him, was just over your shoulder all the while.

They're sending a truck all right, says Donny after stepping back outdoors. Could take an hour or more.

The men debated whether they might stay drinking on the breakwater, wait for Donny's truck there, or make a move. The light was low, their money lower. A man from Clones, name of McCooey, declared that there was only one coast road coming in and out. The truck was bound to encounter them. The walk would pass the hour and save on petrol and give more chance of making The Rock before last orders.

So they did that. They walked through dwindling light on the middle of the road. You'd swear motorcars had never been invented. And we – me, Finny, a smattering of Quay girls – for some reason best known to our younger selves, followed along at a distance of about twenty yards. They were hard men to follow. It was late in the day. There were numerous pit-stops in ditches. Our following involved a lot of standing, waiting for forward momentum to resume. By halfways in, we were astride them and egging them along.

One had a harmonica in his blazer pocket and gave 'Roddy McCorley' a half-time lonesome twang that killed the most of a mile. Donny started on 'Happy Days Are Here Again', but he was sketchy on the verses and nobody else joined in. McCooey, at others' bidding, told of some infamous affray on the platform of Clones station. The others had heard it all before, but wanted to again. Nineteen hundred and twenty-two. A dozen waiting in the waiting shelter, revolvers at the ready. The Enniskillen train comes to a gradual standstill and all these A-Specials alight.

The volleys off of the gunfire would deafen you, says McCooey.

Twenty seconds tops. No longer than that. The platform was covered in pools of black blood. McCooey described this echo ringing. He would never forget it. The echo off of the rifle fire ringing all around the platform. The only sound thereafter was their own footsteps scattering.

We were coming to the T-junction where coast west meets main road north-to-south. We could see Donny's truck ahead.

I did time for that, says McCooey.

Time? asks our Finny. Finny's eyes were massive, the way they got when he got to the best bits of his cowboy books.

Time, says your man. Gaol!

He wasn't being mean. He was more tickled by our big eyes, our greenness. He buried his own revolver under strawberries in his mother's kitchen garden. They came the following afternoon, swore blind, shot hens. They carted him off.

Crumlin Road in Belfast, says he. Year and a half.

His mother was not there when they had come for him. She was in another parish, helping deliver a child. She heard the news on the road home, of her son's taking. She was carrying a basket of eggs given to her for her bother and saw a neighbour running in her direction.

Time, says Finny like he finally understood.

Time, says McCooey. I did time for that.

Donny's truck was parked in the hard shoulder, head-lamps lit. It was a covered cattle lorry with open panels in the sides. The farmers of Armagh and Monaghan climbed up, all weary merriment. The flap got closed. They cheered when the engine started. Their sunken eyes, staring out at us from the sides of a cattle truck, put me in mind of news reels still being shown at intervals in the picture houses. Finny said years later that the same had occurred to him. When the truck started moving, they struck up 'Goodnight Irene' once again. We listened until its chorus had fallen southbound from earshot.

Me and Finny went down and sat into The Duck's front that night. As good as dark. The tide all around. We were neither of us kids anymore. But we had this habit of forgetting, he and I, as long as we were out in the Quay and the given moment lasted, that we were grown men and no longer wild lads snaring rabbits for ferrying across the lough. We sat in the front of The Duck and imagined German bullets spraying down the bank.

I'm thinking New York, says Finny at one point.

Is that so?

Going to New York, says Finny, and finding Ines and making a go of it.

Très bien, says I.

Ines was the Austrian girl whose family had lived in an old schoolhouse on the land of Quakers up the mountain. She and Finny had courted in secret, run away and been caught. The family got visas for America.

Finny was always doing that. Finny was always declaring grand schemes. To me. He was going to buy his very own trawler. He was going to Vancouver. He was going to write all manner of adventure books that would get converted into motion pictures.

A class of sadness fell on me there at the steering wheel. Up to a point, I had believed every one of my brother's schemes. I believe that point may have been that night, when we sat in the front seat of The Duck and looked ahead as if at the rainswept coast of Normandy, and Finny spoke of heading to New York to find the Jewish girl he had courted for two nights in a boarding house in Skerries, and of making an honest woman of her.

The tide was gathering around.

If do, says I. We should make shapes before we're out of our depth.

Some men from a breaker's yard in Camlough came and opened The Duck's bonnet and cranked stuff. Nothing doing. Camshafts melted. Good for nothing but scrap. A crane would have to be sent. A crane was never sent. The Duck sat in the middle of the strand the last few weeks of that summer. Swimmers dived off it when the tide was up and around. When the tide was out, you could see how deep The Duck's wheels were sinking into the sand.

The Duck was there the following spring. The winter tides had pushed it further up the bank. Its lower half was coming apart with the rust. Our Finny invoked the old maritime law: vessels abandoned at sea are fair game.

In this, it seems, he was correct. Finny waited for the next delivery of a railway carriage and paid the crane driver a little extra to winch The Duck up onto our land and there it sat, its nose buried into bramble. It may be there yet, for all I know.

There was a time when we were going to get The Duck running again. Our Francis was back from America, with all manner of plans to rebrand the Quay as a world-class maritime resort called 'Mountain Bay'. Finny would captain The Duck to The Rock and back, and manage the new bar Francis was building. I was to write off for parts. I didn't write for parts, but I may have let my brothers believe I had. I was in university then. I had moved away. I knew enough of Finny's schemes not to act upon them. They came high like the tide, and went out again as quickly and with much the same regularity.

Any word from them suppliers in Wisconsin? asks Finny every time I was home.

No word, says I.

Chase them up, says he. Mark the letter urgent.

I'll do that.

Francis went back to America. Finny sold The Duck's wheels and tyres. Bramble and fern and cow parsley grew around. We unhinged the rear flap and fixed it as a ramp to walk up onto the flat. One good summer in the early fifties, we put up there a tin picnic table and chairs, a few plants in pots, and generally treated The Duck's standing area like a patio or a decking. Many the tea we ate on it.

On a Sunday afternoon, we listened to football matches on the wireless there.

An item falls from the use it was intended for, say, and you stop remembering what it is. It stops being the thing it was. You stop seeing it even. This happened The Duck. Minus wheels, The Duck sunk into the long grass, faced into the ditch behind our railway carriage at the top of the bend above the south shore. Its stencilled **DUKW US MARINE CORPS** wore off the sides. The juice of trodden blackberries, the white of gull droppings, ate into its paintwork. I forgot what it was. Our father did too. Only Finny remembered.

This day ten years ago, says Finny.

Finny said that out of nowhere one of those summers. June, the season not long commenced and the darks as shallow as anything. We were having pickled beetroot and sliced ham roll.

This day ten years ago? asks Dad.

This day ten years ago, says Finny.

Finny patted a segment of The Duck's metal flank that was still visible. We had no clue what he meant.

This day ten years ago, says Finny, this baby was climbing a French beach under heavy artillery.

Is that so? asks Dad and laughs into his plate. Good man, Confucius!

Dad had taken to addressing Finny by Confucius whenever Finny tried to talk about anything more than tide times or the crop of new potatoes. Finny could be, it was true, given to idle hyperbole. You had to see around the side of half of what he said. But that half-truth bled into the whole truth of the other half of what he said. In the end, even when Finny was merely repeating matters of record, verifiable fact, Dad treated his words with the same amused suspicion.

If you say so, Confucius! says Dad. Tell us another!

This Duck saw action in D-Day, says Finny. Nothing surer.

Ah now Fintan! We don't know that, says Dad.

It's peppered with dents from bullets, says Finny raising his voice.

Dents from bullets! says Dad.

Dad had this way of looking at me while countering Finny, and of speaking in plurals. This way Dad had meant that Finny could have his daft assertions all he liked. The rest of us right-thinking people would carry on believing something else. It drove Finny bananas. Without opening my mouth, I found myself repeatedly included in Dad's plural. Such as that night. Finny was staring at me. How was I, his stare said, saying nothing? How could I sing dumb yet again?

For all we know, says Dad looking at me and laughing, that's just the spray off of loose gravel.

Spray off of loose gravel! says Finny rising to his feet. Have you gone blind now as well as deaf?

Dad stayed eating, concentrating intently on what was on his plate. I did likewise. Finny stood and banged his own plate so hard off the table that scraps of food bounced momentarily into the air.

So fuckin sick of this fuckin place, says Finny fully shouting now. You all manage to ignore history, says he, even while you're fuckin sitting on top of it and stuffin your stupid faces.

If you say so, Confucius, says Dad quietly and continuing eating.

I thought Finny might clobber our father. He paused above, fists clenched. Dad even appeared to brace himself for a blow that never came. Finny turned on his heel and jumped down off The Duck and clattered around inside and went drinking in McCrystals'. After the clattering had fallen silent, Dad laid fork and knife side-by-side.

That was not unpleasant, says Dad with regard to the tea. Cat got your tongue?

No, says I. Just wiped.

Sea air will do that, says Dad clearing the table. The sea air will wreck you.

Finny spent that night in the Malone cottage at the end of the back shore. John Malone Esquire was in the home and Finny had the key for looking the place over. That was the first night Finny stopped by himself down the back shore. He stayed below in the Malone cottage thereafter. Nobody said boo. From then onwards my brother was out on a limb. I couldn't ever reach him entirely, however often I tried. I found myself, by default, by virtue of singing dumb once more, among the sea of faces of right-thinking people staring back.

I walked up that bank, years after. It was out of season. I was home from London, visiting Finny down the back shore. Our plot was long sold to people who had replaced the wooden carriage with a bungalow. But the rear was only partly landscaped, there was a scrap of field and fragments of dilapidated machinery still amidst the ragwort, and there was The Duck's back end visible in amongst the bramble. You would have no iota what it was, had somebody not told you. It resembled more a reaper-binder that gave up the ghost in the Depression era. I got close enough to thread my hand through the briar and feel along The Duck's metallic flank. It felt dimpled like a golf ball.

Here's us surrounded by the farmers of Clones and environs, at the junction where the shore coast road meets the main route north-to-south. You can see how dusty the road's surface is. You can see Donny O'Shea's empty cattle truck in the background. You can see, in the top left corner, the edge of the bay and a strip of the coast that would take you south to Dublin. The last of the light is directly behind. We are silhouette. We are shapes just, faces you can hardly make out.

Bronagh McAtasney lives outside Newry, County Down. She is a public historian and curator of the Twitter account @NrnIrnGirl1981 which recounts her childhood journal. She has worked with archives and outreach programmes at the Public Record Office of Northern Ireland and the UTV Archives at Northern Ireland Screen.

CHASING BOYS THROUGH WOOLIES AND OTHER WAR STORIES

I am a blow-in. No matter how long I live here or try to assimilate, I will always be a blow-in. I've lived here now, down near the Border, longer than I've lived anywhere else but I have no roots here, just slight tentacles that cling tenuously to the community. To make things worse, my bloodlines span the Border. A Northern father, a Southern mother. One side steeped in the aftermath of a Border, the other refusing to come anywhere near it for decades. When my mother crossed that line, she effectively disappeared for her family, only existing by phone call or whenever we all went down south. Come to think of it, she didn't really exist in either place, and was not allowed to vote in one place or the other. Up here, everyone asked her where *down south* she came from. When she was down there, they laughed at her northern accent.

Until I was 11, my family and I lived in Holywood, County Down. Then a quaint little town protected from the Troubles by a forcefield of affluence. I could look from my window, across to north Belfast and see the lines of flames, but it was a world away. I remember only two incidents when the forcefield cracked: A bombscare near our school, which meant we all had to crouch behind a wall for a few hours, and the time when a man had been shot and crawled into Mrs Caldwell's garden, only to annoyingly bleed all over her rose bushes which she was forced to clean with disinfectant.

In 1978, my father decided that we should move to Newry. He had been offered a training job, which for him meant the opportunity to pass on his skills as a weaver to young people. Passing on his skills was very important. I'd never even heard of Newry. I knew little about the Border other than it caused problems. I'd seen a photo in a newspaper of a girl tarred and feathered because she mixed with the soldiers and that had something to do with the Border, somehow. I don't remember how we were told about the move. The three of us children had no say in it. One day we were cycling around our cul-de-sac in Holywood, the next we were sitting outside Newry swimming pool waiting for a man to come and pick us up to take us to our new house. Children deal with these big events in different ways. Some accept it all and aren't phased.

Some overthink it and retreat within themselves. I – with my pretensions to be Nancy Drew, or at least an amazing reporter – decided I was going to document my life, and when I got my first diary at 13 (in 1981) this was going to be my moment. In hindsight, I think writing was a way of helping me make sense of things, to put the world in some kind of order, because suddenly life was very very different. The cul-de-sac was gone. There was no garden, no beach around the corner, no park with a Witch's Hat to swing on dangerously. The 'new' house was in fact very old, very smelly and on a busy street with no gardens anywhere; just traffic and noise and big writing on the gable wall that said 'Sniper's Corner'. What was a sniper?

I don't want to write a 'Child of the Troubles' piece. It's more of a 'Life with tinges of violence and an emerald green Triumph 20' thing. In my diary the Troubles are always there just because they are. But we lived our lives relatively unscathed. Bombscares were a nuisance which stopped you going places. Bombs and incendiary fires sometimes provided opportunities for water-damaged bargains or shrapnel souvenirs. For Border people especially, life is all about grabbing opportunities.

Borderlands, hinterlands, shadowlands. Places where laws are simply guidelines or challenges. Where authority doesn't come from the places it does elsewhere. And heroes are the people who get away with things, fighting not so much for what was right but more against being told what to do by people far away.

Teenage life is all about finding your tribe, belonging and sharing obsessions with others. By 13, I had discovered and fallen madly in love with all things Two Tone. My tribe was ska, the '80s kind with distinctly English roots. But the English were also bad, oppressors, tyrants, vengeful. Still, I covered my walls with posters of Madness, skinheads that looked like the soldiers crouched in our doorway. Slowly though, beside the cannibalised pages of *Smash Hits*, other groups of young men began to appear. When Hunger Strikers began to die in 1981, my hero worship became confused. Bobby Sands, Francie Hughes, Ray McCreesh and Patsy O'Hara sat side-by-side with The Specials. When Bobby Sands died, the girls from South Armagh came into school wearing black armbands and I begged my mother to make me one too. Someone gave me a H-Blocks badge and I wore it until my father saw it and tore it off my school blazer in horror. As the summer went on, posters demanding the return of Ireland to the Irish went up and reciting the names of all ten Hunger Strikers became a competition; something that made you cool. I wanted to belong to this gang, rebelling against more than just my parents or school rules. This felt real.

But boys and cycling with your little gang and falling out with schoolfriends was also real. Going down the town on a Saturday afternoon was the focus of our week. Getting the timing just right for optimum running-into-boys opportunities was an artform. Accidentally being in Woolies at the same time as the boy you fancied took precision and organisation worthy of any British regiment. The *will he, won't he* saga of Valentine's cards took up three weeks' worth of pages in my diary and as the year progressed, I had to juggle my dreams to marry Suggs (Plan B was a Newry boy) with my pretensions of being an amazing reporter and Irish rebel. It was a tough balancing act.

On the day Bobby Sands died, for example, I was compelled to report that I had managed to produce edible Cornish pasties in Domestic Science class.

The truth is both of these facts were of equal importance to me. I saw no hierarchy of events. Teenagers don't. In the beautifully insular world of puberty, everything is high drama. How my friends fell out with each other was as vital to note as the bombing of a local hotel or the death of an IRA man. And because I couldn't, or didn't want to, rank the things happening around me, my compulsion was to write it down, the bible-thin pages of my little diary turning solid blue as I crammed in all the news and stories I needed to record in my tiny writing. I made an Irish tricolour out of cardboard and stuck it to the back of my bike only for a boy called Jeffrey to tear it off and throw it in the bin right in front of me. I didn't really know the importance of a flag or a painted kerbstone, but I soon learned.

In 1982, as I grew up, the idea of rebelling took hold. 'Whadda you got?' as Marlon Brando once said. The walls of my bedroom were now covered in posters and stickers. The pop stars and freedom fighters. The diary had gone as I was far too busy going to discos in the Parochial Hall and trying to shrink my jeans skin-tight in a bath of cold water. Lots of storming about, slamming doors in anger and tears. Bananarama and The Wolfe Tones on my record player. So far, so cliché. But it was a lie. I hadn't the true heart of a rebel and I wasn't really a Border person.

I tried so hard. I hung around on the periphery of the cool girls' gang, laughing and nodding along but I could never flick my hair right, and I didn't have that South Armagh – or even Newry – accent and, worst of all, we weren't related to anyone. People couldn't say, 'Oh, the McAtasneys from the Meadow?' and then use that shorthand to place you because of your grandfather or your aunt and the industry your family worked in. I longed to have even a second cousin in the town so people knew who we were. It was bad enough to have a surname no one had heard of, but to come to Newry from Belfast, to have parents from two different places, each child born in a different county, was just too much. We were an unknown entity.

Worse was to come. The opportunity to show my real rebel potential soon presented itself and I was found to be severely lacking.

One Saturday night in October 1982, we were gathered around the TV, doing that most '80s of things: watching the snooker. The snooker was huge. Everyone watched the snooker. When the doorbell rang, I went to the front door and looked out the spyhole to see who it was. Everyone watched the snooker and had a spyhole in their front door. I didn't recognise the fella so I didn't open the door and went back to get my Daddy. When he came back in, the man was with him and he was carrying a gun.

He was very calm for a man with a gun. He didn't have a mask and he simply told us that our house was needed and that we'd all be OK. He said there'd be more fellas along soon and then he just ... sat down and watched the snooker. When the doorbell rang again, more men came in. Six, maybe seven. Some masked, some not. The one in charge explained that they had to use our house for an 'operation' and it would all go very easy if we did as we were told. He knew Daddy was from Lurgan and talked about a recent incident up there. One fella sat beside my brother and when he found out what school he went to, he asked about a few of the teachers who had been there when he was. It was all strangely easygoing. I made them the tea they asked for and we stayed in the sitting room as they ran up and down the stairs.

As the evening went on, they explained that we'd all have to sleep in the same room as they were going to stay overnight in readiness for the attack they had planned for the next morning. Someone had worked out that an RUC car sat outside our house every Sunday morning and that was their target. I needed to get my nightdress and I was allowed to go up to the top of our five-storey house and into my bedroom.

So set the scene. The house is full of masked gunmen. There's snooker on the TV. A massive gun sitting on a tripod in my bedroom. Belts of bullets lying across my Snoopy duvet cover. The Madness and Hunger Strikers posters alongside more recent additions condemning British occupation. Pierrot wallpaper and sullen teenagers. That's all quite Troubles-by-numbers. I'm actually embarrassed by the entire setup. They'd definitely cast James Nesbitt in a drama based on this lot. Probably squeeze in a few poorly-done generic Northern Ireland accents. I'd be played by a young-looking thirty-four-year-old.

It all came to nothing. It would be a different story had anyone been injured or killed. The RUC car didn't turn up. The worst things that happened was Daddy snoring all night, and the men taking our car and cutting the phone. If the attack had gone to plan, the news story would have said that two men with South Armagh accents took over a house and carried it out. That's what they told us to say the previous night. That taught me to never believe a news story again.

How did I fail as a rebel in all this? My posters. My posters gave the IRA men a false sense of who I was. The head fella came to me for a chat. 'I see your posters. Good girl. That's what we need. You know, if you ever want to really make a difference, there are plenty of people you can talk to. Wouldn't it be great to be part of the cause?'

It wouldn't, I thought. My stomach dropped. I wanted to run upstairs and pull them all down. I wanted to say that I just wanted to belong. I wanted the girls in school to think I was one of them. I knew I could fake it enough to be in the gang, but I definitely didn't want to shoot anyone or die. When it came to real commitment, I couldn't do it. I wanted to marry Suggs far more than I wanted to fight for Ireland. I was terrified they'd make me and scared to death that they'd figure me out. Over the next few years, people I knew did make the choice. Some died. Some went to jail. I wondered if they really felt passionate enough to commit to the cause or just found themselves facing the same options I did.

I took the posters down. None of us told anyone what had happened. I could have and it probably would have bumped my chances of getting in with a tribe, but I knew that I was a fake. I decided rebellion wasn't really my thing and focussed instead on music and making lists of the charts which were reliable and not life-threatening.

A few years later I moved back to Belfast for work. Cities are so much easier to belong to because you don't have to belong at all. Ten years after that, I moved again. This time to the US, but it wasn't really for me. There, the Irish people I met seemed to have become more Irish the further they moved. I could have gone full Foster and Allen and lived a happy life of shenanigans (probably in a bar called Shenanigans) but instead came home and ended up living outside Newry in rural County Down. I still don't belong – I fling about words like 'slurry' and pretend to be a culchie but I'm not. I coo at the lambs where my neighbours see their dinner.

Newry still dances along the edge of legality and knowing about a man who can get you that *thing* you want. The Border is there and not there. My sister married a Newry man and I can belong vicariously through his name. I've probably become a Borderlands zealot, feeling the need to prove my credentials by learning about its history, but I don't think I'm fooling anyone.

Michael Hughes grew up in Keady, County Armagh. He is the author of the novels *The Countenance*, John Murray (2016), and *Country*, also John Murray (2018), which won the London Hellenic Prize and was shortlisted for the EU Prize for Literature. He teaches creative writing at Queen Mary University of London.

MARCEL MARCEAU

No point looking. Nothing to see. Not a damn thing. No wall nor fence. No line, no sign, no hut. You might notice the white lines. The speed limit. That's about it. You wouldn't know you were anywhere at all if you were dropped down in the middle of the road. Except nobody ever is. They only ever come up here looking for it, just to say they've been.

Stand right there, and you can feel it. That tingle. The line has been long enough on the map, stretched tight through the place itself, down the middle of us, ourselves, that it's found its way inside the air. Inch along until you find the exact spot. One leg on each side, and you feel it pulling at you, both ways at once. The nearer you live, the better you know that sensation. Some people can't keep away for long. Like sailors and the sea. Lost without it. But it's not everybody can take it. A bit of a dare among young fellows of a Saturday night, half cut, to see who can stand in that spot the longest, before you feel like you're tore in two. Some can hardly talk about anything else after, raring to have another go. And others will knock heads if you so much as mention the thing again.

A different story with the soldiers. Let's say one of them accidentally on purpose gets himself lost, crosses to the wrong side. Chasing after a hood, or just for badness. They aren't fit for it for long. More than a few yards, they start to feel a kind of buzzing. Too far in, the head will be splitting. One time a lad ran the wrong way in total confusion, and he actually cracked down the middle. Wee bits of him left crumbled on the ground. That's what you're up against. That's the force of the thing. But not for us, of course. We feel nothing, nothing at all, once we're over that line. And the other side it's the same, only different. Any of the guards who dander across will melt. Just a bit soft to begin with, but then the whole lot of him starts to slip and drip, and if you don't heed that, soon enough there's nothing only a puddle and a pile of uniform, with a bit of steam rising. Rare enough it goes that far, of course. But you can see the odd one in Dublin, where they've been moved after the unfortunate incident, with a half-melted face. A bad business.

Cross on a Sunday or a Holy Day of Obligation and you might find a priest waiting to skite you with holy water. The wee stick, the bucket, the works. If you duck, or put up an umbrella, the wipers on when you're driving, the altar boys will pull you over and quiz you. Maybe whether you put a capital letter when you refer to that part of the world. And if you say you never write it down, they ask you to speak it out loud, and make their own judgement if there's a capital letter in your voice. Or they try and trick you into saying it, to see will it be the Six

Counties, or Northern Ireland, or Ulster, or whatever. The Republic, or The Free State, or Éire. The penance is different for each one. Three Hail Marys, or a decade of the Rosary, or walk a mile in your bare feet.

For a few years, a good while ago this was, anybody filming for the TV would notice a funny thing when they watched back their tapes. One side was black and white, but the other was colour. Even now, the place over beyond will still look very fuzzy from here, a sort of snow in the air, sometimes a hiss on the sound, until you actually cross. Then if you point your lens back, it's the same the other way. And here's another funny thing. Camera or no, you can't see any action across that line. If there's an incident on the other side, it's kind of invisible. A blast or a bang just won't be heard. However it is, the noise or the fuss or the claiming and blaming just doesn't make it over. Which is part of the point, if you want my opinion. That's the beauty of it.

Once in a while the whole thing is locked down, no traffic either way, whatever the reason might be. That doesn't stop people trying, of course. If a thing is there to be messed with, you mess with it. But anybody who manages to get over is put into a big catapult and fired straight back. That's from the far side. If you're caught going the other way, you have to crawl over again on your stomach while writing out a hundred times I Will Not Try And Cross When I Have No Business. Ruin whatever you have on you. You think twice the next time. That's all for a first offence. If you're a repeat offender, well. Let's just say nobody tries a third time. But some of them will surf it. Take the flag of the opposite side, tie it around yourself, and run right along the line, as close as you can. Fierce energy off it, trying to repel the flag. Magnetic. And if you get up enough speed, you can lift your feet off the ground and scoot along for a few hundred yards. Point them ahead of you, like a child on a slide, and the slipstream might take you a mile or more. Great crack altogether. Though the flag will be ruined by the end of it. Wore thin.

A certain individual told me one time that if the whole thing is ever called off, and the guns and ammunition have to be disposed of, they're all to be dug into the land, right there. Every rifle and bullet and block of Semtex and coil of wire laid out end to end in a line and buried, the whole way across, from Carlingford to the Foyle. Three hundred odd miles. Any that's turned up after will just appear to be an odd one that went astray. Nobody will put two and two together. Nobody would think to look hard at the thing itself, right under their nose. Hiding in plain sight. And all ready and waiting, just in case.

I've heard tell that at the very beginning, when it was first in place, you could see the fairies and the little people on the far side, gathered to welcome you. But they would pop like a bubble if they tried to get over themselves. The stuff they're made of is so fine, it can't stand the disruption. They'd hang around on the edge all the same, looking for mischief, if they thought there was anything afoot. They couldn't help it. Always great men for the crack. Later on, I'm sorry to say, it was sport for the soldiers to stamp on them if they found one. You would see them squashed in the road, if you were driving across, the green oozing out of them, and the troops would always make out like a car had hit them, but you knew rightly. And they knew you knew rightly. That was all part of it.

But they'd be got back. Three brothers one time pulled up a chunk of the thing itself and took it home. They kept it in their roof space, and there was a hell of a stink with guards and soldiers running about bumping into one another, not knowing which side they were on at all. The lads had great crack watching the lot of them chasing their tails. And then they felt bad. It was only supposed to be a bit of a laugh, but the whole place was in danger of falling in on itself. Shops were taking both monies, and the mobile signals were cancelling each other out. The dye was hopping in and out of the diesel, the tags were on and off the ears of the livestock, people were talking in a strange halfway accent, part Paddy, part Billy. It was no way of going on. Nobody knew where they belonged. You can only say you're here when you know you're not there.

So they put it back. And while they were at it, they decided to dig down to see how deep it went. I often wondered if you could go all the way into the centre, a straight line, and then over a degree or two, like a clock hand, one tick, and then out again, just as a straight line, would you come up on the other side. But these lads thought, if it only goes down a few feet, they could tunnel under the whole thing, and that way you would avoid all the fandango, and be over with a clear conscience. Nothing to cross through, because underneath, the land would be all one. But the further down they dug, the worse it got. All sorts was below. All sorts. I won't say, but you can imagine. And the last thing you wanted was that kind of business up to the surface again. So they let it be, and filled up the hole.

Those boys knew no better. Nobody alive remembers the day it was first put in, but you can look up the old newsreel. A remarkable feat of engineering. A whole company of sappers stitched it in there, steel cable and a giant needle, sewing the line through the land. It was fitted up to a generator and an electric current passed through. That ran for forty days and forty nights, a good round number both sides could agree on. To burn it into the land. Scar tissue. A zigzag tattoo. Then the soil of that strip was taken out, and then Border itself was hammered in, big blocks of it. Heavy stuff, shipped from God knows where. That would have been a great contract to have. No shortage of demand for Borders that time. They knocked it in deep as you like, all the way down. Line after line after line of it. 'Til there was nothing below it. A wall sunk into the earth. Then lime poured on top. Quicksilver next. Gold, silver and platinum layers. Fierce strong. The pressure there would be intense. It has to be, if you think of it. Enough to divide a place in two. To keep the two halves of a thing apart. Not easy done. And you'd have some job getting it out again. The top part could be lifted up fair and handy, but you'd never be finished pulling away every trace of it. Never mind the rest. Rumours they brought in a certain individual to curse the spot, with an animal sacrifice. All the way round, the blood was run. Dripped out along that line, across the county boundaries. And when it was done, everybody in the place had to gather along it, and point at the spot, and chant, *There's the Border, there's the Border, there's the Border*. We all have to do it still, every year on the anniversary. To make sure. To make sure we know it's real. Because otherwise you might think there isn't anything there at all. Not a damn thing. And we'd be only a crowd of Marcel Marceaus, bumping ourselves against nothing, palms up, patting along. That bit where he would pretend to push. One leg behind, the other bent forward. Get your back into it. Make the noises of grunting and straining, but the effort is really going into the ground. To keep you in the one spot. Never moving an inch. But there's not a thing in your way. No wall nor fence. Nothing at all. It's just you, all on your own, doing it to yourself, and the rest of them laughing their heads off.

Acknowledgements

It takes a village to write a book, or in cases such as this one, an island. This book was born of the frustration myself and other Border writers felt with the Brexit narrative which was being allowed to dominate the Border region's beauty and vitality. All of us are so much more than local colour vox pops on BBC News, and I'm sure readers will agree that the writers included here prove as much. So I'd like to begin by thanking every one of the writers involved in this project. You've created something of lasting importance and it was a privilege to be your first reader for these pieces.

Special thanks are due to Stephen Reid, without whom I never would have been able to take *The New Frontier* over the line. Stephen had the foresight, knowledge and creativity to shape this book into what it is, and I am grateful to both him and Aoife Walsh for taking a punt on a mad idea. I'd also like to thank Caoimhe Fox, Mariel Deegan and the entire New Island team for all the hard work they've done. Special thanks are also due to Niall McCormack whose design for the book has turned it, not only into a lasting literary document, but a beautiful object to be cherished and passed on.

Thanks as always to the Arts Council of Northern Ireland (and in particular, Damian Smyth), without whose generous SIAP and book funding this anthology would never have been conceived. Thanks also to the folks at the Irish Writers Centre in Dublin, for introducing me to so many talented Border writers during my XBorders residency in 2018, and for providing the space and guidance needed to begin early conversations about this book.

Thanks to Nicholas Allen, Jean Bleakney, Danny Denton, Martin Doyle, Patsy Horton, Tim Jonze, Anna Leszkiewicz, Tim MacGabhann, Martin McConigley, Tara McEvoy, Stephen O'Neill and Robert McLiam Wilson for publishing articles, sounding me out, having the chats and pointing me in the right direction on Border-related topics.

Thanks to my wonderful agent Niki Chang.

Thanks to my parents Conor and Geraldine, my brothers Seán, Joe and Eoghan, and all my extended family for keeping me sane. Thanks to my hometown of Newry for nearly making me *in*sane.

Thanks to my faithful dog, Thelma.

Last word, as always, to my partner-in-crime, love of my life and soon-to-be-betrothed Aimée Walsh. Love you.